INDIVIDUTOPIA
JOSS SHELDON

www.joss-sheldon.com

First published in the UK in 2018.

Cover design by Marijana Ivanova.

Edited by Amanthis, Lis Van Der Wilt, Rae Z Ryans, Rugared, Stern Ceai and Writing Avalanche.

Proofread by David Malocco and Aleksandar Bozic .

THIS IS NOT A PROPHECY
THIS IS A WARNING

WELCOME TO INDIVIDUTOPIA

Perhaps I should start at the beginning.

No, that really wouldn't do. I must start this tale a long, long time before it begins.

You see, between your era and mine, here in the year 2084, the world has changed so much that it would be remiss of me not to bring you up to date. I fear, beloved friend, that the adventures of our hero, Renee Ann Blanca, wouldn't make much sense if I didn't provide a little context.

It may not surprise you to learn that the world will change dramatically over the course of the decades you're about to experience. You live in times of unprecedented change yourself. But to understand the world you'll live in tomorrow, you need to look backwards, not forwards, to 1979, and the election of Margaret Thatcher.

Thatcher's ideology can be summed up by a single, prophetic quote. That short statement, a mere seven words long, would change the world forever.

It's hard for us to imagine Margaret Thatcher as she spoke those seven words. Very few of my contemporaries have ever seen a picture of the *Iron Lady*. People these days are far too occupied with themselves to pay attention to anyone else. I do have an image in my mind of the former PM, although I can't be sure if it's correct. To me, she's a colossus; half-machine, half-human, with a helmet of metallic hair, shoulder pads made of steel and a tongue which could fire off bullets.

I digress. The way Thatcher looked is of no importance. We should be focussing our attention on those seven prophetic words. Those seven, tiny words, which weren't in the slightest bit true, which had never been true, but which would become the only truth there was:

"There"

Thatcher's voice pierced. It was a vinegary screech. It was an autocratic squeal. Poetry without colour. A shadow without light.

"Is"

A static hush buzzed between words.

"No"

A distant footstep failed to echo.

"Such"

A gasp was swallowed.

"Thing"

A camera flashed.

"As"

An eyelash fell.

"Society"

"There is no such thing as society. There are individual men and women, and there are families. And no government can do anything except through people. And people must look after themselves. It's our duty to look after ourselves."

With these seven words, the *Cult of the Individual* was born.

During the decades which followed, everyone would be forced to join.

By the time our hero was born, in the year 2060, Thatcher's claim had become a reality. There really was no such thing as society. Our Renee was all alone.

***

I've read back through the rest of this chapter, and I'm afraid to say that it does get awfully political. Beloved friend: Please accept my heartfelt apologies. This book is no radical manifesto. I actually quite like this Individutopia of ours. It's the only world I've ever known, and I'm rather attached to it, if the truth be told. No. This is a riveting yarn: The tale of one woman's path to self-discovery.

Do skip ahead and see for yourself, if you don't believe me. I'll understand. Honestly, I will. Perhaps political history isn't your cup of tea. That's fine. Totally fine. You must be true to yourself. You must be the unique individual you are!

But first, please do take a moment to consider the four seismic shifts which individualism brought about. These will frame our story:

1) PRIVATISATION. Society's assets were sold to individuals, who charged fees for everything. And I mean *everything*.

2) COMPETITION REPLACED COOPERATION. Everyone competed with everyone else, twenty-four seven, in a vain attempt to be the best.

3) PERSONAL RELATIONSHIPS DISAPPEARED. People were so focussed on themselves, they ignored everyone else.

4) MENTAL ILLNESS BECAME ENDEMIC. Unable to satisfy their social urges, depression and anxiety became the norm.

***

Are you still with me?

Good! I'll fill you in.

Let's start with privatisation...

Since there was no such thing as society, it followed that nothing could be owned by society. Everything that *was* owned collectively had to be passed on to individuals.

Hundreds of nationalised industries, such as British Gas and British Rail, were given to individual shareholders, who increased prices to recoup their investments.

Internal markets were introduced to the National Health Service, through which work was outsourced to private firms. Schools were turned into academies, which were also given away.

Vast swathes of the nation became *Publicly Owned Private Spaces*: Land that appeared to be owned by society, but was actually owned by individuals. Council houses, once owned by society, were sold off and never replaced. It became illegal to squat in an abandoned building.

When the *Democracy Reforms* of 2041 introduced a market for votes, a few rich individuals bought as many as they needed, elected themselves, scrapped every labour law, abolished the *Competition Commission* and disbanded parliament. Free from government regulation, they monopolised the nation's wealth, privatised the police force and used it to protect themselves.

An oligarch class was born.

Fees for education and healthcare were introduced, and then increased, until they became too expensive to afford. Common land disappeared, national parks became private gardens and every beach was fenced off. Fees had to be paid to walk down the street, breathe the air and speak to another person.

In 2016, Oxfam found that sixty-two individuals possessed as much wealth as half the people on the planet. By 2040, these people owned as much as everyone else combined. By 2060, the year our Renee was born, they quite literally owned the world.

***

Now let's turn our attention to competition…

Since there was no such thing as society, society couldn't be held responsible for our problems. We, alone, were expected to take *Personal Responsibility* and help ourselves. As one of Thatcher's closest allies once put it: "My unemployed father didn't riot. He got on his bike and he looked for work."

That's right: If you didn't have a job, it was up to you to get on your bike and take someone else's! In the age of the individual, we don't cooperate, we compete.

At school, whilst schools lasted, a culture of testing was introduced. Pupils as young as seven were forced to compete against their classmates to achieve the highest grades. Salespeople competed to make the most sales, doctors competed to achieve the shortest waiting lists, and bureaucrats competed to make the biggest cuts. A whole system of mystery shoppers, customer feedback surveys, internet reviews, punctuality assessments and star ratings pitted worker against worker. Everything that could be measured was counted and ranked. Everything else was overlooked.

In the 2050s, the oligarchs created a meta-chart which ranked every individual in the land, and an infinity of minor charts, which measured everything imaginable. These days, there are charts that rank people's appearances, consumption levels, calorie intake, computer game scores, ability to eat, skip and sleep. You name it, there's a chart for it.

Individuals are expected to compete against everyone else, all the time, in every way. And, if they succeed, they expect to be rewarded.

I believe this mentality was born back when you were alive...

Forgetting they'd been helped by society, cared for by nurses and educated by teachers, the early Individualists claimed they were "Self-made": They had competed, had won, and deserved to keep every penny they received. They got their way. Corporation tax was slashed from fifty-two percent in 1979, to just nineteen percent in 2017. The highest rate of income tax fell from eighty-three percent to forty-five percent. Both taxes were scrapped completely in the *Great Liberty Act* of 2039.

The poor, meanwhile, were blamed for their poverty. It was their fault, so the logic went, for not getting on their bike, moving to find work, taking a second job or working longer hours.

The *Department for Work and Pensions* ran campaigns demonising anyone who claimed welfare. Newspapers called for people "To be patriotic and report any benefit cheats you know". Neighbours turned against neighbours, the poor turned against the poorest, and everyone turned against the unemployed. The Welfare State was disbanded in 2034, and the last charity closed its doors in 2042. The disabled, elderly and jobless were all left to rot.

The wage gap grew wider by the year.

When Thatcher came to power, the top ten percent of British employees were paid four times as much as the bottom ten percent. By 2010, they were paid thirty-one times as much.

Real wages began to decline. They were lower in 2017 than in 2006.

By 2050, the richest ten percent of workers earned a thousand times more than the poorest ten percent. But even they were paid less than the average employee had earned in 1980.

Still, no one complained. The richest workers were content, happy to know they were being paid more than their peers. The poorest workers, meanwhile, took personal responsibility, pulled up their sleeves and worked harder than ever before.

***

Rumour had it that some people did try to break free from this *Individutopia*.

Whispers circulated about a rebel clique who, *shock horror*, wanted to live together in a society! Those radicals were derided, called quacks and dangerous extremists. No one knew what had happened to them, if they existed at all, but individual opinions did abound. Some people said they had squatted on an oligarch's estate. Others claimed they had gone to the North Pole, Atlantis or Mars. Most people believed they had died. There was no common consensus and, as people became more distant, such gossip faded away.

People became more distant by the year.

Rather than play sport with other people, the Individualists played computer games alone. They drank at home rather than in the pub. They communicated via the internet, instead of talking in person. They stopped saying "Hello" to the people they passed, turned their heads to avoid eye contact, and wore headphones to avoid conversation. They touched their smartphones more often than they touched other people.

Schools told their pupils: "Don't talk to strangers". Insurance companies told their customers: "Always lock your door". Announcements cried: "Keep your possessions close".

By 2030, everyone had unique jobs, with unique hours, and nothing in common with their colleagues. By 2040, every trade union had been disbanded. By 2050, every working man's club, community centre, library, allotment and playing field had been sold off to the oligarch class.

Forced to relocate, in order to find work, the generations split and the family unit crumbled. Fewer people got married, more people got divorced and fewer babies were born. People focussed on themselves. They chased fame, fortune and beauty. They joined gyms, gorged on makeup and became addicted to cosmetic surgery. They only posted their most flattering pictures to social media, and often edited them to make themselves appear more attractive.

By the early 2040s, everyone was a mixture of plastic and flesh, and everyone owned a screen that augmented their image in real time. Everyone believed they were the most beautiful person alive.

People stopped hugging each other. Then they stopped touching each other completely. They wore *Plenses*; computerised contact lenses, which edited a user's vision so they didn't have to look at anyone else. They spoke to their electronic devices instead of speaking to real people. Words such as "You", "We" and "They" fell out of use. There was only "It" and "I".

Thatcher's dream had become a reality. There really was no such thing as society.

The last human-to-human conversation took place between our hero's two parents, just moments before she was conceived. That act of copulation was the last time two adults came into physical contact.

Renee Ann Blanca, in case you were wondering, wasn't raised by her parents. She was raised by the *Babytron* robot which found her in front of the Nestle Tower. Renee's mother believed baby Renee should take personal responsibility and raise herself, so had left her there to apply for a job.

***

Phew! We're almost ready to begin.

But before we do, let's just take a couple of minutes to consider the nation's mental health…

Isolated, forced to do jobs that offered little meaning, hyper-perceptive to corporate expectations, and often owned by the very possessions they'd worked so hard to own, the Individualists were far from happy. By 2016, a quarter of British people were suffering from stress, depression, anxiety or paranoia.

These mental illnesses had physical effects. They raised people's blood pressure, impaired their immune systems and increased the chances of them suffering from viral infections, dementia, diabetes, heart disease, strokes, addiction and obesity.

By 2016, over twenty percent of Brits had suffered from

suicidal thoughts, and over six percent had attempted suicide. Suicide was the most common cause of death for men under forty-five. By 2052, it was the most common cause of death in the nation.

Testosterone levels reduced in men. Women stopped menstruating.

Still, the Individualists refused to look outwards, at the social causes of their mental illness. There was no such thing as society, and so society could not be to blame!

The Individualists looked inwards and blamed themselves. They took personal responsibility, tried psychotherapy, neurosurgery and meditation. Then they took drugs. Antidepressant use doubled in the ten years leading up to 2016, and continued to rise thereafter. People became addicted to sleeping pills, mood stabilisers, tranquillisers and antipsychotics.

When the atmosphere became too polluted to breathe, people were forced to buy their own supply of clean air. Vaporised antidepressants were added to the mix. Our hero, therefore, was born in a druggy haze; high on a mixture of whatever Valium and chemical serotonin her Babytron robot could supply. It was a haze from which she had never escaped.

Over the course of her life, Renee Ann Blanca concocted her own individual mixture of drugs, replete with her own individual flavour: Sour cherry and toffee. Although she reduced her dosage at night, not a single minute passed in which she wasn't medicated. This was probably for the best. These days, individuals usually kill themselves as soon as their gas runs dry.

It all sounds rather morbid, does it not?

Please bear with me. There's a reason I've decided to recount the story of Renee Ann Blanca. It's not nearly as bleak as you might think. But to explain why, at such an early juncture, would surely ruin the tale!

Speaking of which, I suppose we're just about ready to begin.

And here is Renee herself. Yes, I can just about make her out. She appears to be waking, coughing on the drug-filled air which is swirling around her pod.

AND SO WE MEET OUR HERO

"(Slavery) is to work and have such pay,
as just keeps life from day to day."
PERCY SHELLEY

"Renee! Renee! Renee!"

I'm listening to our hero's personalised alarm. Her own voice, recorded many years ago, is calling her into the day.

I'm watching on, transfixed.

Renee's hair is lapping against her pillow as she turns, throwing golden-brown locks against pink cotton. Some crystallised mucus is dangling from an eye which has been disfigured by an excess of self-applied Botox. Her left cheek, the one she hasn't embellished with plastic, is beginning to morph; turning from salmon to puce to beige. Her bandy legs are crisscrossing beneath the duvet, like a pair of industrious scissors.

Here is a star-shaped birthmark on her lower lip. Here is a bean-shaped scar. Here is an eyebrow which has been over-plucked, patched up with artificial hair, volumized with gel and highlighted with pink eyeliner.

Perhaps you can see her too. Perhaps you can see the way she flaps at a screen to stop that alarm. Perhaps you can hear her cough, as her pharynx does battle with this cheap air. Renee can't afford soft mountain air from the Alps, or blossomy air from the New Forest. She must make do with this hard, recycled air, which has been filtered from the London atmosphere itself.

A holographic screen floats fifty centimetres in front of Renee's right shoulder. It's made of translucent pink light, with an opaque orange border, but it doesn't have any sort of substance or weight. Renee can see through it, but can't escape the information it displays at all times.

On the first line, Renee's debt is flashing in a large, red font:

£113,410 and twelve pence. And now, thirteen pence. It grows by a penny for every twenty breaths she takes.

On the second line, in a smaller font, is Renee's position in the *London Workers' Chart*:

OVERALL RANKING: 87,382nd (Down 36,261)

And on the third line, in an even smaller font, a series of minor charts are appearing one after the other. Renee has just climbed twenty thousand places in the Sleeping Chart, leapfrogging Paul Podell. She has an imaginary rivalry with that man, even though she's never met him. She's never met anyone, in the flesh, but this make-believe rivalry gives Renee a reason to live.

She falls below Podell in the Waking Up Chart:

"Me damn it!"

Her charts rotate:

Snoring Ranking: 1,527,361st (Down 371,873)
*** 231 places below Jane Smith ***
Twisting & Turning Ranking: 32,153rd (Up 716)
*** 5,253 places below Sue Wright ***
Saliva Control Ranking: 2,341,568th (Up 62,462)
*** 17 places above Paul Podell ***

"Yes! I did it!"

***

The speaker hummed:

"I'm the only I, better than all I-Others."

Hearing herself recite this mantra always put Renee in a great frame of mind.

Of course, it was a brazen lie. Renee wasn't "Better than all I-Others". Over eighty-seven thousand people were ranked above her in the London Workers' Chart. But Renee wasn't the sort of person to let an inconvenient fact get in the way of a much-loved fiction.

She justified her belief in her own way: Telling herself that eighty million people lived in London, putting her well within the first percentile, which was the best percentile, which meant she was the best. She had topped the Head Tapping Charts for a full three seconds, back in 2072: She would be a chart topper for the rest of her life. And anyway, she was always top of the "Great Renee Rankings"; a chart she created herself.

Her mantras played on:

"I must dress, think and act in a unique fashion."

"I can't have something for nothing."

"I am what I own."

"Too much of a good thing can be wonderful."

"I shall be happy at all times."

I think Renee must have been listening to one of her hypnopaedia recordings during this particular night, because she suddenly jolted upwards and said:

"Ah yes, grass is blue."

Renee had made a collection of recordings, covering everything from astrology to horticulture, music and dance. Their content tended to be quite untrue. Grass isn't blue. It never has been and probably never will be. But Renee believed it wholeheartedly. Since she'd never spoken to anyone else, her views had never been challenged or corrected.

This isn't to say Renee didn't receive new information from external sources. From the moment she awoke, her avatars bombarded her with a constant stream of facts and figures. Some of these were extracted from the internet. Some were true. But this information was personalised; gathered from the sources Renee chose, edited to fit her individual preferences, and supplemented by her own propaganda. It confirmed everything she already believed.

Her favourite avatar, I-Green, spoke in a voice identical to Renee's; bodacious, with an undercurrent of smugness and a hint of girlish frivolity:

"The Great Renee Rankings are in, fresh off the press, and it seems that I, Renee Ann Blanca, am the greatest being alive. Go me! I'm a superstar."

Renee flicked the mucus from her eye.

"Today's job-forecast: Competitive with a chance of hourly work. A low-pressure front is due to creep across the west of town in the early afternoon, so be sure to pack some overalls, and be

aware that there's a ten percent chance of a sacking storm at dusk."

A fine mist of Prozac atomized above Renee's head. She sucked it down and smiled. Ten pence was added to her debt.

"Sale! Are my avatars old, ugly or tired? Am I ready to upgrade to the latest, most super-duper model? Well, come on down and visit www.AvatarsAreRenee.me to get myself a brand new avatar today. What am I waiting for?"

Renee turned to I-Green and grinned. The corners of her mouth reached upwards, dragging her chin towards her nose, and revealing a set of teeth which had been cleaned, bleached, polished, buffed and whitened.

Like all her avatars, I-Green was a digital copy of Renee herself.

Renee's avatars were made of *Solid Light*. You could walk through them, but you couldn't see through them. They didn't glow, like normal holograms. They were perfectly lifelike, with contoured skin and flowing hair.

Renee's avatars all looked like Renee, acted like Renee, sounded like Renee, and said the things which Renee wanted to say or hear. Between them, they satisfied her need for companionship; helping her to take personal responsibility for her social urges, without coming into contact with anyone else.

I-Green was Renee's favourite avatar. It was created on one of those sunny days when everything turns to gold. A good hair day, when Renee earned more than she spent, was promised three whole days of work, got the top score on her favourite computer game and had cheese on toast for dinner. The very sight of I-Green reminded Renee of that happy day. It looked just like Renee had looked back then, wearing a green dress, covered in sequins and pearls. Its cheeks weren't damaged by plastic surgery and its eyes weren't damaged by Botox.

"Special Offer! If I walk down the Old Kent Road today, I'll only be charged three pence per hundred steps. There's never been a better time for me to visit the statue of my dear oligarch, Sheikh Mansour the Fourth."

Wishing to clear some space in her pod, Renee tapped a button and I-Green disappeared.

Almost everyone lives in pods. They're all slightly different, to reflect the fact that their tenants are all slightly different, but they all have one thing in common: They're all incredibly small. House prices rose so much over the last hundred years, that successive generations were forced to move into smaller homes than their parents had lived in. Houses were split into flats. Flats were split into single-room abodes. These abodes were divided, subdivided and partitioned.

Renee's pod was just over two metres long, one metre wide and one metre tall. It was coated with imitation metal and illuminated by hundreds of LED bulbs. A plastic mattress took up three-quarters of the floor, covering a hole which served as a toilet, drain and sink. On the ceiling was a tap which could be used as a shower, although water was so expensive that Renee seldom used it. Showering sitting down seemed like more effort than it was worth.

Along one side of the pod ran a digital screen. Along the other side ran a shelf, where I-Green had been lying. At one end of this shelf were Renee's clothes, shoes and hairclip; a small device which amassed data, took photos and generated Renee's holograms; her display, avatars and virtual possessions. Renee defined herself in terms of what she owned, but couldn't afford many real things, and so collected virtual possessions instead. The only other physical items on that shelf were a small quantity of food, a large quantity of cosmetics, a toaster, a knife, a kettle, and a microwave which Renee had repaired using a fuse from her Babytron robot.

Oh no! Please don't judge our Renee harshly! It's true she dismantled that robot just as soon as she could survive without it. I suppose you might find that a little ungrateful. But Renee had no concept of gratitude. She had never experienced it herself. Her robot was malfunctioning. It seemed to Renee that it was in her best interests to keep its useful parts and discard the rest.

Renee tapped her screen.

I-Sex appeared.

I-Sex looked like a boyish version of Renee. To make it, Renee had cropped her hair, undressed, and used makeup to shade her cheekbones, eyebrows and nose.

Renee activated her virtual penis, beard and flat chest. She swiped these holograms into position, with a nonchalant flick of her wrist, and commanded I-Sex to lie down.

She removed her knickers, placed a pillow between I-Sex's legs and began to grind away.

I-Sex played along.

"Oh yeah!" it squealed. *"Give it to me Renee. Oh yeah! That's the way I like it. I know me girl. Oh yeah! I da best. Wahoo!"*

An ever-thickening mist of sex hormones filled the pod.

Renee panted, sucking down a sharp rush of chemical oxytocin, which went straight to her hypothalamus.

"Right there. Yeah, that's the spot. Yeah, Renee, yeah!"

The chemical dopamine in the air mingled with the natural dopamine in Renee's blood. Trillions of intoxicating molecules surged towards her brain. A cascade of chemical and electrical reactions sent sparks ricocheting around her skull, rearranging the interior reality of her mind.

£113,411.43

£113,411.73

£113,412.03

Renee's heartbeat accelerated. Her breathing deepened. Her uterus contracted, convulsed, and flushed with waves of orgasmic delight. Vaginal juices trickled down the inside of her thigh.

She collapsed through I-Sex and landed with a thud.

"A dastardly virus is coming after my avatars. It's the terrorists! The terrorists! The Obliteration Virus threatens my very existence. Oh, how could I live without my lovely avatars? What would be the point of going on?"

Renee pressed a button on her screen and I-Sex disappeared.

She hated it when I-Sex transmitted information immediately after intercourse, it ruined her high, but she couldn't afford an advert-free model.

She jabbed at her screen, navigated to the Amazon store and

bought some virus protection. Five pounds was added to her debt.

She tapped her screen again.

Renee's unique, personalised blend of perfume filled the pod. It was a perfectly vile blend of cinnamon and camphor, adulterated by a whiff of manure and a hint of rotting ham. No one had ever told Renee that she smelled disgusting, and so she believed she smelled divine. Ignorance, as they say, is bliss:

"Smelling good! Now let's dress to impress."

Renee's clothes were all made by Nike. *Everyone's* clothes were all made by Nike, who bought the competition and established a monopoly back in 2052. This is the thing with individualism, please understand: Everyone has to be different, of course, but their differences must conform. Everyone must wear different clothes, to be an individual, and everyone must personalise their clothes, to outdo everyone else. But those clothes must all be made by Nike. There's simply no choice in the matter, and no one can conceive of a world in which an alternative might exist.

Renee owned two of everything: Two pairs of underwear, two dresses and two bras. She'd added sparkles to her shoes, which had different coloured laces. She'd torn her shirts, added patches to her trousers and invented a stick-woman logo, her own personal brand, which she drew on everything she owned.

She looked down at a Nike swoosh:

"Just do it. I'm going to do it!"

She applied polish to her nails, foundation to her face, gloss to her lips and mascara to her eyes. She tied her hair in a braid, attached her hairclip and tapped the screen. A holographic bowtie, golden necklace and floral brooch appeared in mid-air. Renee swiped them into position:

"Well, one really must create a new, individual look each day. I'll never wear the same accessory twice!"

A sudden surge of duty rushed through Renee's veins:

"I must work, work, work. I mustn't shirk, shirk, shirk!"

She was about to leave home on an empty stomach, restrained herself, and gobbled down some vitaminised toast-substitute; a rather cardboardy affair, which contained all the goodness of toast, but little of its flavour.

She ate a spoonful of foetal jam.

This food was disgusting and Renee knew it, but she just had to have it.

When Nestle monopolised the food supply, back in 2045, they began to use a form of advertising known as *Perception Without Awareness.* Let me explain: Imagine you pass someone who's whistling. You're not *aware* of their whistling, but you soon find yourself whistling the same song. Your subconscious had *perceived* that tune and inspired you to act.

The logo for Nestle's vitaminised toast-substitute consisted of two purple ribbons. The previous day, Renee had viewed several purple ribbons whilst playing a virtual-reality game. She completed a crossword which included all the letters in the words "Vitaminised toast-substitute". Her virtual accessories included a yellow ribbon and a purple sash.

Renee wasn't *aware* of these things, but her subconscious had *perceived* them, and now she felt compelled to eat that toast. Even though it gave her little pleasure, it just felt right.

She rocked as she ate. Renee always rocked as she ate. She believed it was her own individual quirk.

Her stomach rumbled.

Taking personal responsibility for her hunger, she tapped the screen, opened her mouth to the air vent and swallowed down a vaporised hunger-represent. She put on her Plenses and gas mask; a transparent device, which covered her entire head. It contained a microphone, a set of speakers, a drawer-like slot for food, and two tubes. One tube filtered the noxious air, for a price, making it possible to breathe outside. The other supplied a steady stream of antidepressants.

She was ready to face the day.

***

As soon as she crawled through the hatch, four avatars appeared by Renee's side.

I-Green, I-Original, I-Special and I-Extra all spoke out together:
"Obliteration virus successfully shielded. I've been saved in the nick of time."
"Go me. Wahoo!"
"The terrorists want to kill me."
"For the highest chance of employment, I should head to Oxford Circus."
"The terrorists want to steal my precious things."
"The terrorists want my kettle."
"My hatch will get smashed."
"Lock the hatch!"
"Lock the flipping hatch!!!"
Her avatars were reflecting Renee's own personal anxieties.

She panicked, sucked down some antidepressants, recovered, closed her hatch, rotated it, double-locked it with a key, triple-locked it with a security code, added a padlock and added a bike lock:
"Ah yes. I think I'll head to Oxford Circus."
"What a spiffing idea!"
"I couldn't have come up with a better plan myself."
"Gee-whizz, Renee, I sure am swell."

Renee was standing on a ledge, which had flapped open as she crawled outside. Made of perforated metal, it was as wide as her pod, but only sixty centimetres deep. Two of her avatars had no choice but to hover in mid-air.

This didn't stop them from speaking. Renee's avatars were always speaking; complimenting her, echoing her thoughts and supplying her with new information. She was always surrounded by voices, even though those voices were all her own.

The lift zoomed sideways, added five pence to Renee's debt, and opened its doors. Renee entered, descended eighty metres, and stepped out into *Podsville*; a vast expanse of pods, which stretched from Euston to Holborn to Bank. The oligarchs had transferred everyone into this estate, soon after they bought all the land in Britain.

Renee's avatars guided her along an alley which ran between

two banks of pods: A dark, shady artery, where everything seemed to be sucked in towards a distant beam of light. The walls themselves looked like God's own mortuary cabinet; a grid of scratched silver squares, which extended as far as the eye could see. The floor glistened with electric light. Made of old fashioned paving-slabs, it felt a little too clean for comfort. The sky was impossibly distant. The darkness was impossibly close.

£113,418.01

£113,418.02

Renee's debt increased by a penny for every twenty steps she took.

She took large, bounding steps, to get maximum bang for her buck; traversing those alleys at quite some speed:

"Want it now, need it now, demand it now, consume it now."

"I must work, work, work. I mustn't shirk, shirk, shirk!"

"The fastest bird gets the worm."

Renee steamed ahead.

Steeliness responded to steeliness. Smog fell from the sky. The light slept, comatose; appearing to be in a different, faraway world, right up until the point at which it burst into life.

It blinded our Renee and caused her head to spin.

"I should turn left for Oxford Circus."

Renee turned left, stumbled around I-Original, and almost tripped over a dead cat.

I-Extra feigned injury and I-Green winced.

Renee nudged the cat aside with her toe:

"Damned useless I-Original. It's as if I'm trying to get in my way. I should've gotten rid of I years ago."

Renee had grown to despise I-Original. It was the first avatar she'd bought, back when she was four. Whilst its personality had updated, amassing new data, based on Renee's thoughts, actions and speech; its body had remained the same. I-Original was just ninety-seven centimetres tall, with pigtails and freckles. It struggled to keep up, and often got between Renee's legs. Even though it couldn't possibly trip our Renee, or be hurt by her, Renee still felt compelled to allow I-Original its space. It was as if she was moved by a duty to care for her younger self.

She hated that! She hated I-Original. It was a constant reminder of how weak and feeble she had been.

She sucked down some gas and muttered her favourite mantra:

"I'm the only I, better than all I-Others."

And then:

"Better than my avatars. Better than I-Original. Better than I was when I was four. Better than ever before!"

This improved Renee's spirits, although she couldn't help but take one last swipe at I-Original:

"Oh, keep up, will I? I haven't got all day."

I-Original gave Renee a salute and sprinted ahead.

They bounded through Russell Square, a concrete expanse, hidden beneath the Nestle Tower. That factory produced enough food to feed the entire population of Podsville, brewing synthetic meals in giant vats before delivering them by drone.

Like most of the buildings in this part of town, the Nestle Tower was made of aquamarine glass. The panels at the bottom shone so brightly they gave our Renee a headache, but they faded as they rose. One hundred stories up, the Nestle Tower was more black than green. After three hundred stories, it was lost in the smog that hung above London like a wig: Toxic, wispy and grey.

£113,418.38

£113,418.39

She galloped down Montague Place, passed an oligarch's townhouse, in what was once the British Museum, and mocked the other avatars in the street. Renee didn't look at those avatars. She didn't listen, touch or smell them. She couldn't even be sure they were avatars, and not real people. Her Plenses edited her vision, making people look like avatars, and the speakers in her gas mask often removed their voices. But she was vaguely aware of their presence, and was sure she hated them all.

"This one's got a beard!"

"What sort of female grows a beard?"

"*This one's all flabby nostrils and clammy skin.*"

"It's a jelly-nosed sweat-bucket if ever I viewed one."

"*And this one: It's so sunburned it looks like an orange!*"

"Fluorescent hell on earth! Orange juice on legs! Oh my."

Hurling insults was Renee's favourite pastime, and it was I-Special that always egged her on, describing the avatars that Renee mocked. I-Special was made when Renee was feeling holier than thou, having just been named *Worker of the Day* by Balfour Beatty, and the residue of that superiority lingered on in its programming. It even looked supercilious. Its locks were made of thick golden light, its bandy legs were stretched taut and its back was held straight. It looked down on Renee's other avatars:

"*This one's monobrow looks like a giant slug.*"

"Like a great, big, greasy slug! Stupid avatar."

"*Full of hot light.*"

"Hot, stupid light."

"*With a maggoty-mouth and a puggish stare.*"

"Puggish! Yes, puggish!"

Oh, you're judging our Renee, aren't you? Beloved friend, I think you are! Well, I'm not going to defend her. Her mockery didn't become her. But do try to see things through her eyes. Renee had never met another person. She didn't know if they had feelings, and had no idea how to talk to them. She was unsure if anyone was listening. Since she couldn't hear anyone else, she assumed they were being quiet. This made Renee want to be noisy, to be different, like a true individual. And anyway, she didn't care. Mocking avatars made her feel great, which saved her a fortune on antidepressants. She expected everyone was at it, although not as well as her. She was only saying out loud what people in your day might have thought to themselves. And some avatars really did deserve to be mocked. These days, avatars are all either perfectly weird or weirdly perfect. I'm not sure which are worse.

Take this one, here. Can you see it? I can only just make it out it myself, with these brown corduroy trousers, tied up with string, and these shoes which have more scratches than a carpenter's bench;

with this cherubic, shiny face, which doesn't quite fit this body, and this braid, which sways with every motion.

Whilst its torso was fixed in a rigid position, its hand was inside its trousers, jerking back and forth. Brown corduroy thudded like the beating of a terrified heart. Eyes clenched tight with lusty fervour.

The wind seemed to whisper her name: "Rah... Rah... Renee?"

But Renee wasn't listening. She was too busy masturbating herself.

"It's wanking in public! What a nonce!"

She tutted, shook her head and upped the pace. She bounded through Bedford Square, passed the *Monument to the Invisible Hand*, galloped down Tottenham Court Road and turned onto Oxford Street.

Once a shopper's paradise, where glitzy displays wooed the passing punter, Oxford Street had long since been swallowed up by the *West End Industrial Estate*. The last shop closed its doors when Amazon became the monopoly retailer, selling everything online and delivering it by drone. These days, there aren't any shops in London. There aren't any pubs, cinemas or parks. There aren't any trees. They were removed because they didn't generate enough profit. There aren't any birds. They left because there weren't any trees.

Instead, the streets are filled with an infinity of colourful figures, be they avatars or people. It's just a pity Renee never noticed them, if you ask me, because they all looked rather splendid.

This one was dressed as a goth. That one was dressed as a hippy. These ones were dressed as mods, bikers, punks, hipsters, nerds, ravers, rude boys, surfers, hip hoppers, glam rockers, skaters, soulboys and trekkies. Those ones were dressed as clowns, witches, nuns, vampires, dandies, hags, jocks and drunks. They were wearing every colour under the sun. They came in every shape and size. They were all true individuals, with their own unique scent, haircut, cosmetic surgery, walking style, mannerisms and characteristics.

If you were to visit this postmodern incarnation of Oxford Street, you would surely be wowed by the sheer splendour of these individuals. Behind them, you would see the old brick facades with which you may be familiar, saved for posterity, or nostalgia, or because no one bothered to knock them down. And, rising above these first few stories, you would see row-upon-row of aquamarine towers.

Each tower had its own individual sound.

Renee's ears were besieged by the jabbering of mattress-making machines in the Ikea Depot, the tapping of number-crunching computers in the Visa Tower, and the ribbetting of the Samsung Column.

The noise was incessant:

Click-Clack

Tip-Tap

Yip-Yap

"Renee's eyes are so green."

"This building was built by Martians."

"Selena Frost earned thirty-three pounds working for Veolia."

"Dildos! Dildos! Dildos! Get myself a Rampant Rabbit today!"

£113,418.64

£113,418.65

Renee had arrived in Oxford Circus.

***

The nature of work has evolved over the course of the last century. Jobs for life were replaced with short-term positions. Zero-hour contracts became the norm. Those contracts became shorter each year, and were scrapped in 2047.

Without guaranteed employment, individuals have no choice but to search for a new job every day; competing with their peers to win whatever piecework the oligarchs are willing to give them.

This is why Renee found herself here, in front of the Podsicle Interviewer.

This avatar was a reflection of the oligarch who owned Podsicle Industries. It was programmed to follow that man's commands, but not to display his humanity.

Please don't be misled! The oligarchs' avatars may mine data from another person's avatars and use it to reflect *their* personality. They may issue instructions based on the corporate goals of their corporations. But they don't display any character or emotion. They're purely rational, but not at all reasonable. Talking to an oligarch's avatar is like talking to a computer. It can't be considered a substitute for real human contact.

One thing, however, was certain: The Podsicle Interviewer was handsome, oh so handsome. A finer specimen, humanity has never known.

It reflected an oligarch who must have been constructed from luxury muscle: Flat-chested, broad-shouldered and long-limbed. The harsher angles of its body seemed to have been sanded down, smoothed and softened. Its skin glowed; all terracotta, silk and enamel. It was frightfully clean, as though it had been pampered, groomed, manicured and massaged on an almost hourly basis.

This avatar's demeanour conveyed a blissfully unconscious sense of supremacy; reflecting an oligarch whose superiority came so naturally to him, he didn't find it in any way conceited. He simply *was* superior, just as a cat simply *is* feline, and a bird simply *does* have wings. Fact.

The Podsicle Interviewer stared off into the distance, indifferent to Renee herself. The buttons sparkled on its tailor-made suit. Simply being in its presence was enough to evoke the aroma of peppermint and honey.

But it was handsome. Oh, so handsome. I can't emphasise this enough.

It logged Renee's details, using an augmented version of Renee's own voice:

"Renee Ann Blanca. Worker 2060-5446. Aged twenty-four. Debt: £113,418.65. Worked for two hours yesterday. Masturbated at twenty-three minutes past seven. Only had one slice of toast for breakfast."

Renee responded as though she hadn't noticed the avatar's good looks:

"Present."

She didn't say anything more. Renee was charged twenty pence for every word she said to an oligarch's avatar, and knew from experience that adding superfluous words wouldn't improve her chances of winning a job.

"One slice of toast? How in the name of the market is that going to supply enough energy to do a good hour's work?"

"Experience."

"Hmm, let me take a look at the data. Yes, the numbers show that this breakfast has been consumed on two thousand and sixty-seven occasions. An average of two hours and thirty-three minutes of work has been completed after such a breakfast, generating an average wage of twenty-six pounds and thirteen pence."

"Exceptional!"

"I can work for so long, for so little."

"I'm the best employee in the world."

The Podsicle Interviewer smiled.

Renee scowled.

"One really must work hard. It's been scientifically proven that for every ten calories burned at work, a wage is earned which is large enough to buy at least eleven calories of food."

"That avatar doesn't deserve to find work before I do."

"Birth rates rose again last week."

"Invest that income in calories. It'll provide fuel for more work, which will generate more income."

"There's no business like the Babytron business."

"So how many calories can Renee burn for Podsicle Industries today?"

"I should apply for a job with Babytron."

"My debt could be erased with 6500 payments to Visa Repay."

"This paving slab is made of jade."

Struggling to cope with this bombardment of information, Renee could only stutter:

"Lots… Ah… Ah… All!"

She winced.

"Eighty pence," she thought. "That's how much this job

application has cost me: Eighty frigging pence! Why did I have to say 'Lots'? I've blown it now. 'All' was the right answer. I knew it. I just knew it. I should've said 'All' to begin with."

She sucked down hard on her gas.

"*I wonder if it'll give me work.*"

"*It doesn't know when it's onto a good thing.*"

"*I'd be better off working elsewhere.*"

The Podsicle Interviewer paused, bit its lower lip and made a "Hmm" sound:

"I'm afraid this application hasn't been successful. But be proud! Renee was better than ninety-nine percent of interviewees. Congratulations! Bravo!

"It'll be an honour and privilege to provide some feedback: This brooch could be positioned a little to the right and these legs could be held a little straighter. Work on that and do feel free to reapply in an hour. That's one hour. Not thirty minutes. Not two hours. One – Renee – hour.

"For the good of I."

"*For the good of I!*"

"*I'm the best.*"

"Pfft! I-Original isn't the best, giving my thoughts away like that. Bloody me! I cost me my job and eighty pence."

Renee laughed the insulting laugh of a jackal and inhaled some antidepressants.

This is what she always did when she failed to win a job: She blamed her avatars and inhaled some gas.

Shifting the blame onto her avatars, even when she was at fault, was Renee's skew-whiff way of taking personal responsibility. Since her avatars were digital copies of Renee, blaming them was much like blaming herself. It was a deeply cathartic process, which eased her nerves and soothed her emotional tension; allowing her to accept her faults, whilst continuing to believe she was perfect.

Sucking down on her gas injected a rush of antidepressants into her bloodstream. It made her feel amazing, and put her in the right frame of mind to apply for another job.

Renee wrote enthusiastically on her holographic notepad: *Hold my legs a little straighter. Return in an hour. Babytron job sounds like a goer.*

She repositioned her brooch and headed to Great Portland Street, where she was interviewed by one of Babytron's avatars; a squat thing, with a faulty light drive and a baggy face. Renee paid it no attention. She only said two words during the entire interview, "Learn-a-riff-ick" and "Perfect", and so was only charged forty pence. But her application was rejected because she'd never worked for Babytron before and so didn't have the experience required.

She applied for another job with Microsoft. The walk to their office cost her ninety-two pence in footsteps alone, but it didn't result in a job.

By the time she returned to Oxford Circus, Renee's debt had increased by over four pounds. Still, she didn't feel down. There was so much serotonin racing through her veins, she actually felt rather euphoric. She genuinely believed she was about to win the job of a lifetime.

"Ah, beloved Renee. Worker 2060-5446. Debt now at £113,422.93. Applied for three jobs already. Walked eight-point-three kilometres in an hour. Bravo! That *is* impressive."

Renee nodded. She didn't wish to pay for a verbal reply when she hadn't been asked a question.

"It appears a job has been earned. Congratulations! Here's what Podsicle Industries can do for Renee: It can offer an unpaid internship. There are no guarantees, but if the intern's performance is in the top two percentiles, it could result in a full five hours of work. Think about it."

Renee didn't think about it.

"I'll do it!" she screamed. "Yes I will!"

One pound and twenty pence was added to her debt.

Her avatars cheered.

The Podsicle Interviewer continued in an uppity tone:

"The internship will take place on Dallington Street, in Clerkenwell. Not in Dallington, New Zealand. And not on

Darlington Street with an "R". *Dallington* Street."

Renee scribbled on her holographic notepad: *Dallington Street. Not in New Zealand. Not with an "R".*

"But hurry. This internship isn't guaranteed. Positions will be awarded on a first come, first served basis."

Renee scribbled: *First come. First served. Hurry.*

She underlined the word "Hurry".

"Oh," she thought.

"Hurry!"

"Chop-chop."

"That worker will get there before me!"

Renee gave chase.

Taking those long, loping strides of hers, she bounded past the Apple Dome and the Bank of China Debt-Processing Plant, turned up Tottenham Court Road, lost the avatar she was chasing, turned into Bedford Square, passed the Monument to the Invisible Hand, mocked the masturbating avatar, thought she heard her name, "Rah... Rah... Renee", convinced herself she hadn't, and re-entered Podsville, passing her pod almost three hours after she'd left it.

Her avatars glowed, illuminating a path through those labyrinthine alleys.

She exited Podsville, bounded down the Kings Cross Road, passed the Johnson & Johnson Acre, and arrived on Dallington Street.

Glassy towers rose like demonic stalagmites, imprisoning our Renee beneath the grey smog above and the grey concrete below. A three-dimensional billboard span above her head; advertising cola, pensions and mascara; turning from red to green to blue. On one side of the street was a giant letter "I", worn with age, which shaded half of Renee's face. On the other side was the Podsicle Empire; a mammoth building, covered in millions of stickers, which each said "Human Free Zone".

Renee panted, lifted her arms to the sky and left her avatars to cheer:

"I made it!"

"Go me!"

"Whoop-dee-doo."

Her avatars guided Renee towards the Podsicle Supervisor; a carbon copy of the Podsicle Interviewer, with the same chiselled shoulders and glowing skin.

Staring off into the distance, it spoke in a voice which did nothing to hide its lack of interest. It was as if it was following a computer program, which, of course, it was:

"Renee Ann Blanca. Worker 2060-5446. Debt: £113,424.73. Pulse: Ninety-seven. Respiratory rate: Thirty-nine. Perspiration: Four. Disposable calories: One thousand and sixty-seven."

Renee waited for more, but this avatar had a glitch. It flickered, spluttered, said something inaudible, and finally continued on:

"This internship will involve a series of tasks designed to generate kinetic energy for Podsicle Industries. Here at Podsicle, the generation of kinetic energy is taken very seriously indeed."

Renee nodded.

"The internship will consist of the following: Three thousand hops, two thousand skips, one thousand squat-thrusts and thirteen head pats."

"Thirteen?"

"Yes, thirteen. What a splendid number of head pats! Renee will fail the internship and receive a Compliance Rating of zero if the head isn't patted exactly thirteen times. Not twelve times. Not fourteen times. *Thirteen times!* Podsicle Industries has a zero-tolerance policy when it comes to insubordination."

Renee nodded with gusto.

"Ah, head nodding. Yes, that *is* good. Two bonus points shall be added to Renee's score. Well done. Bravo!"

Renee beamed. She was loving this job already.

Of course, she wasn't producing anything of value, but Renee *never* produced anything of value. She didn't have to. These days, everything is produced by machines, automated by computers and transported by drones. Work exists to keep people occupied; to ensure they're too busy to rise up and overthrow the oligarchs. It's meant to be a challenge: People want to work more, so they can earn more, and then consume more. They want to be better than their peers, top the charts and earn their bosses' praise. Work is meant to be addictive: Fuelled by a fear of failure, and charged by the rush of success, it offers people the chance to kill time; to escape their lives, feelings and thoughts. But it isn't meant to be productive. Oh no, beloved friend, oh no!

Renee smiled. Relieved to have found a job, she dreamed of earning a paid position, and worried that her debt would become unmanageable if she did not.

Her avatars counted her hops:

"*Seventy-something.*"

"*Three hundred and a bit.*"

"*Six hundred and lots. Yippee! Look at me go!*"

Renee spoke to herself:

"Nothing can be achieved without perseverance."

"A calorie burned, is two calories earned."

"I must prove myself at work."

Sweat flooded her shirt, stained the hem and discoloured her holographic bowtie. Lactic acid flushed through her veins. Her muscles twitched.

She cheered:

"No pain, no gain."

And then:

"The more pain, the more gain."

"*One thousand.*"

Renee performed a star-jump, inhaled, exhaled, and began to skip between a charging robot and the Podsicle Empire itself.

£113,426.14

£113,426.15

She was charged a penny for every twenty skips she completed. By the time she'd finished, she'd spent a pound on this one task alone. She'd spent sixteen pounds since waking, but hadn't earned a penny. Her body was on the verge of collapse and her mind was on edge, but her mantras kept her going:

"Hard work is virtuous."

"I'm so virtuous."

"Oh my."

"My royal me-ness."

"Oh me in heaven above."

Her avatars cheered whilst Renee completed her squat-thrusts and head pats. They nattered as they led her to the Podsicle Supervisor:

"I was so good."

"I've never done a squat-thrust like it."

"Never. And my skips! Hallelujah, praise myself!"

"Oh, shut up, will I? Dearie, dearie me."

Fatigue had made Renee irritable, but she took solace from her rankings. She'd risen by over a million places in the Squat-Thrust Chart and made it into the top ten thousand in the Skipping Chart, although her Adherence Ranking had plummeted as a result of her star-jump.

Seeing this, Renee panicked, sucked down some antidepressants, exhaled and grinned.

The Podsicle Supervisor frowned:

"This internship hasn't been successful. Renee Ann Blanca, worker 2060-5446, was better than ninety-nine percent of interns, but didn't make it into the top two percentiles. However, Podsicle Industries is the best, better than the rest. It's so great, it's going to offer Renee another chance. If Renee can make it to the Podsicle Interviewer within thirty minutes, Renee will win three and a half hours of paid work. For the good of I!"

"For the good of I."

"I'm the best."

Renee was already running.

Her vision was blurring, and she was becoming nauseous, but still she stumbled on:

"Fall down seven times, get up eight."

She removed a half-empty tube of calorie-substitute from her pocket, opened her gas mask's food compartment and began to suck.

One hundred calories... Five hundred... A thousand... Two thousand...

That paste contained all the nutrients Renee required, but none of the flavour one might desire. Not only was it packed full of calories, it was also a rich source of proteins, vitamins and carbohydrates. It tasted of chalk and salt.

Renee gave herself a second to digest her meal, drank some water from a puddle, braced herself, recovered and charged ahead.

***

"Renee Ann Blanca. Worker 2060-5446. Aged twenty-four. Debt: £113,427.88. Internship completed. Arrived in twenty-nine minutes and twelve seconds. Disposable calories: Two thousand and fifty-nine.

"Ah! How very splendid. Yes, Renee is fantastic. Bravo! Podsicle Industries is delighted to offer Renee three hours of work, for a most generous payment of nineteen pounds and six pence."

Renee was so ecstatic, she didn't realise she'd lost thirty minutes of work. She was jumping with joy, grinning with glee, hollering, shouting and spinning.

"Please report to Podsicle Palace, my London townhouse, which is located at the junction of The Mall and Constitution Hill. That's 'The Mall'. Not 'The Hall'. Not 'The School'. 'The Mall'."

The Mall, Renee scribbled. *Constitution Hill. Not Hall. Not School.*

"Renee's first task will be to move the furniture from the Yellow Drawing Room to the White Drawing Room. That's yellow to white. Not yellow to green. Not white to blue. And be careful! This is valuable stuff. This isn't the sort of job that could be entrusted to a machine."

This was exactly the sort of job that could have been entrusted to a machine.

Yellow Drawing Room. White Drawing Room. Don't trust machines.

"When this task has been completed, one final task will be issued."

Completed. Issued.

"Well? What in the name of the market is Renee waiting for?"

Renee looked up, froze, unfroze and turned. She sped down Saint George Street, Bruton Lane and Berkeley Street, before arriving outside Podsicle Palace; a historic building, fronted by Bath stone and red asphalt, which had been the home of several British monarchs. You may know it as *Buckingham Palace.*

The gates opened and Renee stepped through. Oblivious to everything around her, she focussed on her avatars, which led her into the Grand Hall.

A red carpet, the colour of internal organs, was surrounded by an amber glow. Tall mirrors reflected their own golden frames, the regal patterns on the ceiling, and the light trapped inside a hundred chandeliers. Even the white spaces seemed faintly yellow.

A musty aroma, which smelled of the past, mingled with the scent of lavender potpourri. A robotic vacuum cleaner glided across the floor. A humanoid robot dusted a marble column.

Renee forced herself on, before her eyes could acknowledge a thing:

"Slothfulness is a deadly sin."

"Never put off till tomorrow the work I can do today."

"Offer! Mattresses are just one hundred pounds per square metre."

Renee repeated Ikea's corporate slogan:

"Home is the most important place in the world."

She ascended the Grand Staircase, turned down a hall, and entered the Yellow Drawing Room.

Her avatars lit up with flashing arrows, which led her to a painting. She could view every carving on its hand-gilded frame, but couldn't make out the portrait of Queen Victoria itself. Her Plenses had turned it into an image of Renee:

"How jolly delightful!"

"I'm delightful. Yippee!"

Renee tore the painting down, hurriedly, causing some plaster to crumble from the wall.

"Oh me, my son and my holy spirit! Darn blasted I-Original. Why did I have to be so hasty?"

She scowled at I-Original, rubbed the plaster into the carpet and sucked down on her gas. She tucked the painting under her arm and galloped away, without noticing the nodding figurines in their niches, or the Chinese dragons whose necks jolted out towards her. She rushed down the hall, without noticing the mirrored doors or porcelain arches. She didn't notice how the fragrance of that gallery transformed from jasmine to orris to musk.

She focused on her task.

The doors to the White Drawing Room flung themselves open. Renee bounded past a secret door, a golden piano and several armchairs. She followed her avatars to a hook, and hung the painting on the wall:

"Nice girls finish last. This is a win-lose world, baby, and I'm going to win. I'm gonna win the arse off this job!"

She swooped, balletically, and retraced her steps. Then she returned, a full thirty-six times, carrying paintings and ornaments and chairs.

It took her two Renee hours in all.

You see, in this Individutopia, everyone keeps their own time. Renee's days contained twenty-five hours, one more than the norm, because Renee considered herself to be that bit better than normal folk. To compensate, each Renee hour was slightly shorter than most other hours. This did have the potential to cause confusion, but Renee didn't care. She assumed she was right, everyone else was wrong, and she was pretty damn special for putting up with them.

Her legs began to ache.

She sucked down the last of the calorie-substitute. It was a risk. Taking a break, even for a second, was deemed the most heinous of corporate crimes. But there was a rebel spirit in this girl. She thought she could get away with it.

She placed the last of the ornaments atop a fireplace and turned into the Podsicle Supervisor. It was wearing ruby cufflinks and a silk cravat, which made it look like a genuine member of the aristocratic class.

Renee didn't notice. She was too busy admiring her own feet.

"Renee Ann Blanca. Worker 2060-5446. Aged twenty-four. Debt: £113,430.31.

"The second part of this job is as follows: Move the furniture from the White Drawing Room back to the Yellow Drawing Room, and place it in the exact same position as before. That's white to yellow. Not white to green. Not green to blue. In the exact – same – position."

Renee scribbled: *Exact. Same. Position.*

She was off. Boosted by her recent calorie intake, and motivated by her new challenge, she returned the items in three-quarters of the time it had taken to remove them.

The Podsicle Supervisor returned:

"This job has taken seventy-six minutes too long. A penalty of three pounds and twenty pence will be deducted from Renee's pay. A further two pounds and twenty-seven pence will be deducted to compensate for the damage done to the wall.

"Podsicle Industries is delighted with Renee's work. Bravo! Renee is amazing. As a reward, Podsicle will issue Renee with a voucher worth sixty-eight pence. Go Podsicle! Podsicle is the best."

Renee punched the air with delight.

"The voucher will be issued within ten working years. For the good of I!"

"*For the good of I.*"

"*I'm the best.*"

"*A Mars a day, helps me work, rest and play.*"

***

Renee had no choice but to return home. There were no public places to visit, it was dark, and she was too tired to walk much further.

The streetlights came on automatically, charging her a penny for every twenty seconds of light. It was unnecessary, her avatars illuminated the way, but there was nothing she could do.

The rain formed a misty haze that was too light to notice, but too pervasive to miss. It smeared the streetlights across the black backdrop, turned single bulbs into a bleary lightshow, and created a galaxy of star-like flickers amidst even the smallest of puddles.

Renee mocked an avatar I-Special claimed was spitting:

"Disgusting slob!"

Then she spat herself.

Renee often behaved like this: Spitting, littering, salivating, and sneezing without covering her nose. You might call her "Antisocial". But you must remember that there's no such thing as society. It's been extinct for several decades. Calling someone "Antisocial" is a bit like calling them "Anti-Dodo" or "Anti-Aztec". It doesn't make a whole lot of sense.

Renee arrived home, crawled inside, and waited for her screen to come to life. She updated her online profiles, adding her experience with Podsicle Industries, applied for twenty-three different positions and bid for several virtual projects.

Undercutting every other worker, she finally won a job. In return for two pounds and fifty pence, she spent the following hour recording a podcast about the fighter drones of the Roman Empire, believing she was an expert on this fictitious topic.

Her head jutted forwards. There was no escaping her pride.

Not one to rest on her laurels, Renee invested in her future. She spent three pounds to complete a course on *Mumbo Jumbo*, but struggled to get past the first line:

"The Imaginary Gobbledegook Parenthesis states that all teaspoons are greater or less than all Visa, unless the mattress is a shower."

She read this sentence, shook her head, tried again, running her finger across the screen, became frustrated, held her mouth to the vent, inhaled, exhaled, tried again, failed again, sighed, checked the hatch and inhaled some more gas. She repeated this process a dozen times, without making it to the second line.

She updated her CV:

"Qualified expert in Mumbo Jumbo."

She devoured some fake beef, made from rat meat, and some

fake peas, made from dyed soya beans. She washed them down with
an algae smoothie, before treating herself to a Mars bar.

She rocked as she ate:

"A Mars a day, helps me work, rest and play."

"*Mars is a planet.*"

"*Planets are big lumps of chocolate.*"

"*The terrorists! I-Others want to get me!*"

Renee inhaled some gas, opened Alexa and ordered her
shopping: Another tube of calorie-substitute, which cost five
pounds, a lab-built apple, some protein pâté, and three new virtual
accessories: A brooch with a dragon motif, a silk cravat and a pair
of ruby cufflinks.

Her order arrived three seconds after it was completed:

"Three seconds! The efficiency of consumer capitalism never
fails to amaze me. When I was a child, that would've taken a full
eight seconds. And now it takes just three! I mean, wow. That's what
I call progress."

Renee triple locked the hatch, lay down, doubted herself, and
returned to check the lock.

She exhaled, pulled out a set of pedals from beneath her shelf,
locked them into position and began to cycle. This powered the UV
lights in the ceiling, which tanned her to a crisp.

She applied some skin-whitening cream, to ensure she didn't
get *too* dark, rolled over, tapped her screen, and created two I-
Friends; animated copies of herself, that only existed online. Renee
had thousands of I-Friends, all of which liked her tweets, shared her
photos and replied to her posts on Facebook. They made her feel like
the most popular girl alive.

She spent the next half hour flitting from one activity to the
next, without spending more than three minutes on each. She
washed her face, checked Twitter, cleaned her socks, checked
Instagram, played a computer game, cursed herself for not getting
the top score, inhaled some gas, sent herself a text, sent herself an
email, watched her Email Rank improve, checked the hatch and read
an ebook, "Queen Renee The Great", which had been written

especially for her.

She was charged for each activity.

She yawned, sent I-Love a virtual hug, received a virtual kiss, closed her eyes and drifted into unconsciousness.

She was happy.

She'd earned £13.59, after deductions, for her work with Podsicle Industries, and a further £2.50 for the podcast. This gave her a total income of £16.09. A good wage indeed!

She'd spent £38.19, including £8.23 on air and £9.71 on footsteps. She considered this rather frugal.

Renee paid no attention to her debt, which had increased by £24.60. She focussed on her improved rankings, curled up into a foetal position, hugged her toaster and drifted off to sleep; certain she'd repay her debt within a few short years, buy a pod, and retire by the time she turned sixty.

IT STARTED WITH A DRAGON

"Reality is merely an illusion."
ALBERT EINSTEIN

Once upon a time, a girl was on a pilgrimage to Canterbury Cathedral. When she heard a horse, kicking up dust as it cantered down the lane, she called out to the horseman, who she hoped would give her a ride:

"Hey there. Where are you heading?"

The horseman wore a look of confusion:

"*Me*? Where am *I* heading? I don't have a clue where *I'm* heading. You should ask the horse!"

The girl opened her mouth to speak, but the horse had already bolted.

***

This was how Renee felt when a job alert woke her in the middle of the night. One of her applications had been successful, which gave her a momentary thrill.

This sensation didn't last for long. Her mind had already been consumed by the thudding image of a piano.

To Renee, who had never viewed a piano, this image seemed so strange, so unexpected, that she was unable to focus on anything else. Like the horseman, who was beholden to the will of his horse, our Renee was held captive by the mysterious workings of her subconscious mind.

The piano was a thing of beauty.

Apart from its keys, it was completely golden, with brass mounts, incurving legs and leonine paws. The parts not decorated with floral carvings, were covered in monochrome designs; with monkeys in dressing-gowns, banging on drums; lizards in waistcoats, standing erect; frolicsome old-world dancers, winged cherubs and garlanded maids.

"What's this, and why am I viewing it now?"

Even the designs seemed peculiar to Renee, who knew nothing of lizards and monkeys:

"What?... Where?... Why?... Why am I imagining such things?"

Half asleep and bleary eyed, she fumbled about in search of her hairclip; slapping her wrist against the air vent and knocking her head on the tap.

Water sprayed around the pod.

Renee turned the tap off, found her hairclip, dropped it, rubbed her head and activated I-Green:

"What?... Why?... Tables with black and white buttons. Golden mother of I!"

I-Green didn't answer.

I-Green followed a computer program, amassing data, based on Renee's previous behaviour, before applying it to the situation at hand. But it had never observed Renee in such a state, had never known her to view such images, and so had no data with which to build a response:

"*I must teach myself new skills every evening. I-Others don't rest.*"

"*All teaspoons are greater or less than all Visa.*"

"*My dopamine levels are running low.*"

Renee frowned:

"Say that again."

"*My dopamine...*"

"Yes. Err... Yes!"

Renee had set her air vent to supply a lower dose of antidepressants whilst she slept, to save herself money. But she'd been awoken early, when the air was still light:

"That's it: I'm under-medicated."

The piano caressed its own keys.

Renee adjusted her air, and held her mouth to the vent to inhale.

The music played on, mixing delicate rhythms and dainty rhymes. The image of the piano began to fade, the painted designs began to blur, and the carvings began to flatten. All was golden light. But still the music played.

A mythical beast drifted into focus. It's long, reptilian neck swished in a manner which was both speedy and slow. Scales morphed into spikes, which morphed into claws; with no apparent beginning, middle or end. Still the music played. But now there were teeth. And now there was form.

Renee recognized the image:

"But where have I viewed it before?"

"*Viewed what?*"

"A golden beast with... Umm... Triangular claws."

"*My new brooch.*"

"Oh yeah."

Renee opened the virtual brooch she'd bought the previous evening:

"Umm... Hmm... Well, yes. That explains it."

It didn't:

"But why was I viewing the image of a virtual brooch? I've... I've... Oh fudgesicles. I've never been overcome by images before.

"Why now?... Why here?... Why this?...

"Why did I even buy such a peculiar design? Why? It's not like me at all."

The image of the dragon blurred to gold and a new image appeared. Renee's vision was consumed by a nodding figurine. Then a lavish red carpet. Then a crystal chandelier. Then a thousand chandeliers, which each reflected the others.

Renee smelled potpourri, jasmine, orris and musk:

"Why???"

She pressed her mouth against the vent and sucked down as hard as she could:

"Why, why, why, why, why?"

She tore her hair, scratched her scalp, and watched on as ornaments turned into chairs, and then arches, and then paintings.

It hit her, like a slap to the face. She'd finally spotted something she recognized: A portrait of herself in a gilded frame:

"The carvings… The contours… It's so… Umm… Familiar. Where have I viewed this before?… Yes! Umm… Yes! I moved this yesterday in… In… In Podsicle Palace!"

"*Podsicle Palace!*"

"Yes! That's it!"

"*It is!*"

"The table with musical buttons, the beast with a long tail, the nodding statue, the fluffy red floor, the spiky white light, the other paintings… I must have viewed them all in Podsicle Palace."

It all came down to that old chestnut: Perception without awareness. Renee's conscious mind hadn't been *aware* of her surroundings in Podsicle Palace, but her subconscious had still *perceived* them. That, it seemed, had been enough.

The images began to take shape. Renee observed the whole of the Grand Hall. The carpet, mirrors and chandeliers were all in position. The robotic vacuum cleaner was gliding across the floor:

"But it's so… So… So big."

Renee couldn't believe it.

I-Green could:

"*Podsicle Palace contains eight-hundred rooms, two-thousand doors and forty-thousand lights. Its floors cover seventy-seven thousand square-metres.*"

Renee's jaw dropped open:

"Seventy… Seven… But… How many pods could fit inside?"

"*Twenty-nine thousand if placed side-by-side. Over ninety-five thousand if stacked.*"

"Ninety-five thousand?"

"*Ninety-five thousand three hundred and three.*"

"Three hundred and three?"

"*Yes.*"

Renee tapped her lower lip:

"How much would it cost to buy so many pods?"

"*My pod retails at two hundred thousand pounds. To buy ninety-five thousand would cost me nineteen billion pounds.*"

"And how long would I have to work to earn that?"

"Earning sixteen pounds and nine pence a day, I'd have to work for over two million years."

"Two million Renee years?"

"Yes. Have a break. Have a Kit Kat."

"I can't have a break! I need to work for two million years! I'm Renee Ann Blanca: The only I, better than all I-Others. I'm the best! I deserve the best. I deserve Podsicle Palace. I have to have it. I have to have it now!"

Renee smiled with glee:

"I'm going to do it! I'm going to buy Podsicle Palace!"

She turned red, grabbed the kettle and hurled it towards the hatch.

Smash!

"I can't buy it. I can't!"

Pieces of lid, base and casing littered Renee's duvet. The heating element rebounded into the screen, which turned purple at the point of impact, and then blue, and then black. The cord remained in her hand.

Her speech was slurred:

"What else have I been missing?"

She pictured the Grand Staircase, Long Hall and Yellow Drawing Room:

"And what does this mean?"

I-Green was unable to answer.

Renee was besieged by a series of thoughts. Some she uttered out loud, others she did not. She couldn't be sure what she was saying and what she was thinking:

"How could any I-Other afford such a palace? How could it work for two million years? It couldn't have possibly worked harder than me, I'm the best, so how on earth did it buy it? Why can't I buy it? I want it. I want it. Oh, it's just not fair."

She was shocked by her own negativity.

She shuddered, pressed her lips to the vent, sucked down hard, and shouted, hysterically, as if she'd been struck by a divine revelation:

"Personal responsibility!"

"*Hard work is next to me-lee-ness.*"

"Idleness is wrong."

"*I must trust in myself.*"

"I'm going to do it. I'm going to work for two million years!"

She positively beamed. Her cheek, the one not made of plastic, turned from beige to pink to magenta.

She clenched her teeth, ran her nails up her mattress and screamed:

"Aaaawww!!!"

It had dawned on her:

"I'm earning less than I spend. I'll never repay my debt. I'll never own Podsicle Palace."

Her ignorance couldn't save her. Her knowledge was eating her alive:

"No, no, no, no, no!"

She tried to make sense of her situation, shouting, but becoming quieter with each passing word:

"There's no other way. History is over. I live in the best of all possible worlds. I have super-duper gadgets. I find work almost every day. I live in a free country. I'm free! I have my liberty, health and independence. I'm unique. I'm me. Me, me, me!"

I-Green nodded:

"*That's it. I go girl. Look at me go!*"

"I need to calm down. Come on, Renee, calm down."

"*Don't sweat the small stuff. Just do it!*"

"Yes, I'm going to do it. I'm going to do whatever it takes. I shouldn't overestimate something which is so obviously unimportant: These measly facts, which belittle and deceive me. These thoughts! These thoughts are my enemy! I shouldn't let these strange, alien thoughts contradict what I've always known to be true. I shouldn't trust these images of Podsicle Palace, which keep changing and morphing and moving, so it can't be said what's real, if any of it's real at all. It can't be! The truth is what it was, not what it seems. The truth is what it's always been. It's absolute. I'm the truth! I need to be true to myself. To me, glorious me. I'm the way, the light and the truth. I should focus on what's important. On me. On being better than I am. On being better than the best."

Renee viewed the White Drawing Room in all its glitzy glory. She came face-to-face with its lofty ceiling, covered in gold; the carved cherubs, who frolicked above the crown moulding; and the rug, whose patterns zigged and zagged in circles. It all looked so real! Renee felt sure she was standing in that room, running her hand along the mantelpiece and inhaling the perfumed air.

"And my debt!" she exclaimed, as if discovering a shocking piece of news for the very first time.

"*£113,438.49*"

"Oh."

"*My debt could be erased with 6501 daily repayments of twenty pounds.*"

Renee repeated Visa's slogan:

"Everywhere I want to be."

Then she shook her head:

"Six thousand... Six thousand and... But... But I'll never be able to..."

"*I will. I can do it!*"

"No, I can't! I earn less than I spend. I can't make a single repayment. This life has no end. It goes on and on forever. Round and round and round. I'll never repay my debt, I'll never retire, I'll never be... Be... Oh, it's useless."

Renee rolled one way and then rolled back. She clenched and unclenched her fists, clicked her toes and cycled her legs.

She heaved herself up, held her mouth to the vent and sucked as hard as she could.

In. Out. In.

Deep breath followed deep breath, but her antidepressants refused to take effect:

"Why am I even having such thoughts? I've never doubted myself before. I've always been so happy."

"*I shall be happy at all times.*"

"I'm breaking my own rule! But why? I never break my rules. Oh me. Come on! Snap out of it. Be strong!"

She couldn't do it.

The images swirled around her mind. Her thoughts came thick and fast. She clawed at her mattress and thumped the sides of her pod.

As if twenty-four years of suppressed negativity had hit her at once, she found herself winded, choking on thin air, unable to breathe:

"I'm going to end it. I'm going to take personal responsibility for my life. I'm going to take personal responsibility for my death. I'm going to end it. I'm going to end it now."

Everything was clear.

She turned her toaster on, turned it up, grabbed her knife, and lifted it above her toaster's open jaws.

Her heart thudded, heavy and strong:

Boom-bam. Boom-bam. Boom-bam.

Time slowed. Renee's eyes narrowed. The light dimmed:

"I'm free now. Blissfully free."

Her knife moved slowly, steadily, getting ever closer to the toaster's element.

Thousands of EDF volts were ready to jolt Renee's knife, impact her fingers, and shunt every electron in her body; causing so much friction that her heart would spasm, go into cardiac arrest and bring her life to a premature end.

The knife moved closer. Renee's hand seemed to float. She squinted. I-Green closed its eyes.

The knife was just four centimetres from impact. Just three. Just two. Just one...

The toaster glowed.

Here was a fizz of electricity. Here was a taste of the hereafter. Here was an end to the suffering and doubt.

Renee's eyelashes touched.

She shuddered.

She paused.

Moved by some sort of sixth sense, she yanked herself away, hurled the knife over her shoulder and inspected the scene.

It was the vent.

There, in the corner, the tube which dispensed Renee's antidepressants was doubled over. It looked worn, as though it had been bent on several occasions, or with quite some force.

Renee noticed the blood popping out from between her knuckles:

"I must have slapped the vent when searching for my hairclip."

She scrambled across her pod, grabbed her knife, wedged it into the nozzle, levered it straight and squeezed it open. She sucked at her vent for a full ten seconds, exhaled, and inhaled again.

She didn't stop.

Her muscles relaxed, twitched, and then relaxed. Her hands tingled. Her tongue tasted of sugar. She felt light, empty, happy and free.

Her eyelids closed with skittery motion.

She began to sweat profusely.

She drifted into unconsciousness, but not before recalling a story she'd told herself many years before:

"Hang on… When an I-Other stops taking its gas, it *always kills* itself. Always! That happens when it doesn't get work, and so can't afford its medication. *Always*. Always!"

This inspired one final thought:

"I've had a horrible experience. My mind hasn't been my own. But I didn't crack. Where I-Others would have faltered, I pulled through. I diagnosed the problem, found a solution and survived. I'm so much better than I-Others. I'm a bonafide hero!"

Renee focussed on this thought, as every image from Podsicle Palace; every chandelier, mirror and carpet; was pulled out of her mind in a fantastical vortex of light.

Everything was solid black.

Everything was silent.

Everything was still.

***

OVERALL RANKING: 87,382nd (Down 36,261)

Renee awoke with a thudding headache. Her brain pulsated, bashing against the insides of her skull. She dry-retched, lifted her mattress and vomited into the sinkhole.

Her good cheek twitched, spasmodically, without any discernible pattern; shuddering three times, resting, rising slowly, falling quickly, waiting, jerking, trembling, and quivering with a broken-beat.

She shivered. Goosebumps covered her arms.

She vaguely remembered waking up, having some strange thoughts, sucking on her gas and falling asleep. But she couldn't remember why she'd woken so early, or the nature of her thoughts. Her experience had been so unusual, so traumatic, that her brain had blocked it out:

"Headache."

"Serotonin syndrome."

"Sera what?"

"I inhaled too much gas in one short burst."

"Oh. I think I've done that before."

"Seventy-five times. I'm the best. I can inhale so much gas at once!"

Renee washed her vomit down the drain and flipped her mattress back into place. It landed with a thud, causing some fragments of her broken kettle to bounce:

"That's strange... I wonder... Hmm... It must be I-Others."

"I-Others want my precious things."

"Yes... That's it... I-Others want my kettle!"

Renee lunged at the hatch and yanked the lock, only to discover it was bolted. She couldn't quite believe it. She unlocked it and relocked it four times, before cradling her head in her hands.

She noticed the job offer on her screen.

As the timer ticked upwards, the pay-rate ticked down. The job was currently worth one pound and nineteen pence, but it was falling by a penny for every ten minutes that passed.

Despite the low pay, Renee still felt compelled to complete the task. She'd made a commitment when applying for that job, and felt duty bound to see it through.

Skipping breakfast, she began to write a report for Podsicle Estates, typing as I-Green dictated:

"The table with keys was commissioned by Queen Victoria in 1856. Supported by curly-wurly legs, it was decorated with images of furry beasts. Both Prince Albert and Scooby Doo used it to compose concertos. Podsicle Estates bought it for sixteen million pounds."

The idea that a simple object could be worth so much caused Renee a brief pang of discomfort. She couldn't comprehend this fleeting emotion, which vanished as soon as she inhaled, and didn't give it a second thought.

She sent an email to I-Research, an I-Friend she used to trawl the internet for information. She texted I-Data, I-Analysis and I-Clever, waited for their responses, ignored them, made up some new information, and nodded with glee.

She was proud of her work.

She closed I-Green, opened I-Sex and completed her morning routine.

She was ready to face the day.

***

As Renee waited for the lift, she was startled by the sun's sunken position. Its light seemed to slice the sky above; creating a horizontal plane, which hovered above her block, without entering Podsville itself.

"Report successfully completed. I've been paid one pound and eight pence. Go me!"

"Ooh, I'm loving my brooch. What a bizarre design."

"To win myself a job, I should head to Russell Square."

"The immigrants want my precious things."

"Lock the flipping hatch!!!"

Renee inhaled hard, closed her hatch, rotated it, double-locked it with a key, triple-locked it with a security code, added a padlock and added a bike lock:

"Ah yes. I think I'll head to the Nestle Tower."

"*What a damn fine plan.*"

"*Finger lickin' good!*"

She took the lift, bounded through Podsville, repeated some mantras, kicked the dead cat, listened to some adverts and reached Russell Square.

Her avatars were unable to locate the Nestle Interviewer:

"*Interviews will commence in an hour.*"

"I should use that time to look for another job."

"*I'll lose my place in the queue.*"

"I should stay."

"*What a magnificent idea!*"

"Well, yeah. I *am* pretty magnificent, I suppose."

Renee removed her hairclip and used it to take a selfie. She tilted her head, pouted her lips and took another. She lay down, arched her back, looked away and took a third. She got up, leaned forwards, held her foot behind her back and took a fourth.

After she'd taken ten such selfies, she edited them, applied filters, and posted them to Facebook, Instagram and Twitter.

She read her I-Friends' replies:

"*Oh my Renee. O.M.R.! I mean, like, wowza!!!*"

"*Corr blimey. I'd love a bit of that arse.*"

"*Yum! x*"

Renee received thousands of likes, hundreds of hearts and several smiley faces. She spread her legs, took another selfie, and then took a hundred more.

***

Night had descended by the time the Nestle Interviewer appeared. The smog had mingled with the cosmic darkness, forming a melange of black and grey swirls. The ground glistened.

The Nestle Interviewer had a beard that had been clipped and caressed into a stiff dome, as if it wasn't so much a beard, but a facial accessory. This avatar was broad-shouldered, burly-armed, puffed-up, thickset and ever so slightly purple.

It took one look at Renee, uttered eight words and disappeared:

"I don't like the look of this applicant."

Renee could barely speak:

"Don't... Like..."

She doubled over, almost choked, almost swallowed some phlegm, inhaled some gas, and immediately felt better. She read a few comments on Instagram, and immediately felt great.

She made some notes: *Must change appearance when applying for work with Nestle. I'm gonna get a job!*

Buoyed by this sudden burst of positivity, she skipped back home; certain she'd be able to repay her debt, buy a pod, and retire by the time she turned sixty.

£113,451.59

£113,451.60

Her debt had increased by sixteen pounds and eighty-eight pence.

IGNORANCE
WAS BLISS

"If you think adventure is dangerous,
try routine. It's lethal."
PAULO COELHO

Do you ever feel like you're a machine, repeating the same old routine, day in, day out, without stopping to question why?

This is how I find Renee.

I watch her wake. Some crystallised mucus clings to her eye. On this day, it's pale amber. And on this day, it's tangerine.

I watch her golden-brown locks billow as she turns.

I listen to her mantras.

She jolts upwards and exclaims:

"Ah yes, bananas are red."

"Ah yes, frogs have wings."

"Ah yes, BODMAS!"

I can almost smell her. Can you? For sure, the aromas of rotting ham and manure do little to nurture a connection, but the smell of cinnamon already reminds me of her. It's *her* smell, after all. Whenever I drink a cinnamon latte, I immediately think of Renee. Perhaps you're the same. I'd like to think you are. Please! The next time you smell cinnamon, do give our hero a thought.

I prefer not to watch her masturbate. Beloved friend: A man must have some decorum! And yet I feel I must. I feel I must watch on, transfixed, as she dresses, applies makeup, eats, rocks, goes out, locks the hatch, bounds through town, applies for one job, applies for another, retouches her makeup, takes some selfies, wins a job, completes that job, mocks an avatar, snaps at I-Original, returns home, eats, shops and sleeps.

This isn't to say each day is the same. No! Oh no! Every day is unique. *Everyone* and *everything* is completely and utterly unique.

Renee puts on different makeup, in different ways, each and

every day. Her accessories are never the same. She always applies for different jobs and works in different places.

On this day, she finds three jobs. On this day, she doesn't find any. She turns up to worksites where there may be work, where work is advertised, or where she's found work before. She's told to wait, or go away, or complete a form. She's interviewed, or rejected, or recruited.

Nestle offer her a job, at the fifth time of asking, after she's adjusted her appearance in several different ways. She spends eight hours destroying food she'd love to eat, but will never be able to afford; salivating, and then inhaling her antidepressants. Unsure why she's doing this task, she's happy to know she's doing it well, and dreams her work will be rewarded.

She finds a job in a call centre, talking to unsatisfied computers. She's made to smile so hard, for so long, that her jaw begins to ache. It doesn't open for another two days.

She spends a day folding paper, several hours searching for Bigfoot, and a particularly slow shift working as an attendant in an abandoned toilet. She sorts the different rocks in a mixture of gravel, and then mixes them back together. She supervises some robots who refuse to acknowledge her existence. She spends an hour moving data between spreadsheets. She spends a morning on her back, allowing her belly to be used as a launchpad for drones. She spends an afternoon repeating the phrase, "Try turning it off and on again". She stands on a street corner, holding a sign that says "Golf Sale - Turn left". She walks around a fountain, to check it's not on fire. She walks down a road, to check it exists.

She creates adverts that encourage consumers to buy accessories they don't need, clothes they can't afford and cosmetics no one will notice. Then she buys some accessories, clothes and cosmetics; spending far more than she's been paid.

On these two days, she earns more than she spends. On this day, she earns thirty-five pounds. Her debt trickles upwards, but it does so at a slower rate. It's as if she's being rewarded for not questioning the system again; for being smart enough to work, but not smart enough to question why. Or, then again, perhaps she isn't. I shouldn't make unsubstantiated claims. Beloved friend: I do apologize. One mustn't be misled by conspiracy theories.

***

Renee experienced more neural activity each time she fell asleep. Stiff and restless, she began to wake up early, when the air was still light.

Under-medicated, she could sense something was missing, but couldn't be sure what it was.

It was a queer feeling:

One part physical, it produced a lightness in the hands and a dull ache in the ears. She was sensitive to sound and suffered from headaches.

One part mental, it left her wanting to ask questions she couldn't understand. It was as though something was hidden inside her, but she didn't know what it was, where it was, or what she had to do to get it out.

She would turn to the vent and inhale. Her worries would drift away.

But this isn't to say she was happy, merely that she was numb. She needed her antidepressants, just as she needed air and water, but they didn't bring her any joy.

With this in mind, let's return to Renee here, on this vaporous, apricot morning; this blossomy, ethereal, April day.

Outside, a thin, acidic rain is rising up from the ground, forming a cottony haze. The syrupy aroma of wet tar is light and unassuming. Ripples of light shimmer in the air.

Inside, our Renee is in a world of her own; indifferent to the turning of the tides or the changing of the seasons; the wind, rain and clouds...

***

£113,518.03
£113,518.04
OVERALL RANKING: 87,382nd (Down 36,261)
Sleep Ranking: 26,152,467th (Down 7,251,461)

*** *25,161,829 places below Paul Podell* ***

"For my sake!"

Renee shook her legs, rubbed her forehead and turned towards the vent.

She was about to inhale, when she glimpsed a piece of broken kettle:

"But... No... It can't be... I threw my kettle into the alley..."

She picked it up, rolled it between her fingers and explored it with her eyes:

"Why? Why did my kettle shatter? Why? *Something* must have happened."

She put it down and turned to the vent:

"No! I'll never work it out if I medicate. I need to keep a clear head. I need to be strong."

She pinched her thigh:

"No pain, no gain. The more pain, the more gain!"

Feeling nauseous, she gripped the shelf and turned back towards the vent:

"No! Stay strong, Renee, stay strong."

She sat up, placed her head between her knees, placed her fingers on her temples and tried to think:

"What had happened? Why can't I remember? What does it mean?"

It was no good.

She activated I-Green.

"I can tell it's going to a great day. I'm going to have a worldy!"

Renee shuddered:

"No... Just... 'No'... Something's not right."

"Don't sweat the small stuff."

"The small stuff? This might be the biggest problem I've ever faced."

"Calm down and just do it!"

"Calm down? Just do it? Calm down?"

Being told to calm down made Renee even more anxious than before:

"Why aren't I calm? Will I ever be calm? Do I deserve to be calm? Is it important to be calm? What's important? Is anything important? Does anything matter? Do I matter? Does the kettle matter? Why did the kettle break? Why can't I remember? Why am I so useless? Why am I full of doubts? Why am I breaking my mantra: 'I shall be happy at all times'? Why, oh why, oh why?"

Renee scowled at I-Green for the first time in her life:

"Calm down? How could I tell me to 'Calm down'?"

She recalled the day I-Green was created; that good hair day, when she earned more than she spent and had cheese on toast for dinner.

Her angst spoke louder than her words:

"Oh, what childish hope!"

She'd thought that day would mark the start of something special. She'd believed she'd go on to get more work, earn more money, clear her debt, buy a pod, and eat cheese on toast every day:

"And now look at me. I haven't had cheese on toast in years!"

She glared at I-Green, glared at herself, realised how old she'd become and how little she'd achieved.

"*Special offer! If I buy ten mattresses I'll get the eleventh half-price. Go Renee! Go me!*"

She turned red:

"I haven't achieved anything! I want my own pod. I want eleven mattresses. I want cheese on toast for dinner!"

She threw herself at the vent:

"No, Renee, no! There must be more to it than this. These thoughts... I've never... It and it must mean something. My kettle... This plastic... There's... There's something I need to know."

"*The University of Wikipedia has courses on everything I need to know. Subscribe today for just £49,925 a year.*"

"No, that's not it."

"'*It' is a novel by Stephen King.*"

"No, no, no! It's one of my mantras. I was thinking of one of my mantras."

"*I am what I own.*"

"No."

"Too much of a good thing can be wonderful."

"No."

"I shall be happy at all times."

"No. Oh… Hang on… Yes! I'm breaking my own rule. I've not done that before. Or have I? The kettle? No. Yes. Hmm. The kettle!"

Renee leaped towards the hatch, checked the lock, unlocked it, locked it, and tied a shirt around its handle.

She covered her face in makeup, hurriedly, smearing mascara down her cheeks, and placing a virtual eyelash halfway up her forehead:

"I don't believe me, do I?"

"I believe everything I say. I'm just so perfect."

"But I'm not, 'Perfect', am I?"

Renee couldn't believe what she was saying. A stabbing pain zipped across her ribs, her head tipped forwards and her jaw hung loose.

I-Green crashed. Unable to process the information it had gathered, it turned blue, compressed into a two-dimensional form, fizzed and turned itself off.

"Well, I *am* perfect, let's not be melodramatic. But I'm not *so* perfect. I'm far too modest to believe that."

Renee counted to ten, tapped the screen and waited for I-Green to reboot:

"Where was I?"

"My pod is located on level…"

"No, no, no. What was I saying?"

"I'm breaking my own rule. I've not done that before. Or have I?"

"I have! That must be it. I must have been unhappy. Why else would I break my kettle? I must have looked at I-Green, realised how little I'd achieved, and lost my temper."

"I must have."

"Indeed, I must have. And so I must work harder. I must work more. I must buy my own pod. I must eat cheese on toast for dinner."

"*I must take personal responsibility.*"

"I must trust in myself."

"*Just do it!*"

"I'm going to do it!"

***

It was still dark when Renee crawled outside. Those towering Podsville walls were streaky with oily water: Khaki, bluish and bronze. Frost sparkled in the air. Pollution smudged the stars.

Renee's gas mask supplied a higher dose of antidepressants than the vent in her pod, but her breathing remained light and so it had no immediate effect.

"*The unemployed are leeching off my hard work.*"

"Bloody slackers!"

The very idea made Renee fume. Stress hormones flushed through her veins and she almost gulped down some gas.

Her avatars repeated her words:

"*No! I need to keep a clear head.*"

"*The more pain, the more gain.*"

"*To find work, I should head to the Apple Dome.*"

"*The unemployed want my precious things.*"

"*Lock the flipping hatch!!!*"

Renee was about to suck down some antidepressants. She always inhaled her gas whenever I-Special said "*Lock the flipping hatch!!!*"

"No, Renee, no! Just no!"

Her muscles turned to rock. She held her breath, grabbed the railings, counted to three and exhaled:

"Okay, okay. It's going to be okay."

Trembling, with tears in her eyes, it took her several attempts to close and lock the hatch:

"The Apple Dome... I mean... Yes... Maybe... The Apple Dome!"

Renee's legs had turned to jelly. She gripped the railings as the lift descended, and stroked the walls as she walked through Podsville.

She was overcome by paranoia:

"Are the avatars staring at me? Are *I-Others* staring? What if my knees buckle? What if I don't find work? What if my mattress is stolen? What if I can't afford cheese on toast? Why am I worrying so much? It's not normal. It's not right!"

She turned out of Podsville and kicked the dead cat, which had taken on a bloated appearance.

Froth dribbled onto Renee's shoe.

"Bloody beast."

"What sort of thug leaves a beast in the street?"

"A fool."

"A cretin."

"A toad."

Renee stubbed her toe on an uneven paving slab:

"What idiot did that?"

"I'd never do that."

"I'm the best."

Renee felt sensational for two whole seconds. Then her doubts resurfaced:

"Am I the best? Am I perfect? 'So' perfect? Could I make a better path? Could I even make a path? Why haven't I made a path? Have I made anything? Why don't I make things? Does what I do really matter? Why am I even alive? Why, oh why, oh why?"

She forgot each question as soon as she asked it. Still, the dull thudding of doubt lingered on. She felt broken, as though she'd been split into hundreds of tiny pieces and would never be whole again. Every scene seemed more pronounced. This grey concrete, here in Russell Square, seemed luminous and bright. This black wall, by the old British Museum, seemed to possess its own gravitational pull. The industrial growling of the Boeing Engine Plant sounded like a sonic boom. The whispering of her name, "Rah... Rah... Renee", almost registered on her conscience. This fence felt as rough as sandpaper. These windows smelled of chlorine gas.

Yet, despite this hypersensitivity, Renee felt strangely disconnected:

"Am I even here? Am I anywhere? Does anything actually exist?"

The sky seemed impossibly large. This lane seemed impossibly narrow. Her avatars seemed too hollow to be real.

Mentally anguished and physically drained, she doubled over, held her hands on her knees and began to pant. Without realising what she was doing, she inhaled a large dose of gas.

It happened with supersonic speed: The antidepressants took effect, Renee's doubts disappeared and her thoughts turned in on themselves:

"Why aren't I-Others as good as me? Are I-Others as good as me? Am I as good as I-Others? Yes! I'm the best. Am I the best? Yes! I'm fantastic. I-Others are useless. I'm the best. Me! I've always been the best. I'll always be the best. Oh me in heaven above!"

Renee smiled.

I-Special cursed:

"This avatar has a bony face and lopsided cheeks."

"Is it gormless? I bet it's gormless. I bet it's got bandy legs."

"Yes! And this one's got a blue moustache. It's mouldy!"

"Mouldy? Oh Renee! It must stink! If only it smelled like me."

COULD IT BE REAL?

"If there's anything worse than knowing
too little, it's knowing too much."
GEORGE HORACE LORIMER

In the mid-1950s, the members of a cult, *The Seekers*, were told to sell their homes, divorce their spouses and quit their jobs, if they wanted to be saved from an apocalyptic flood.

They gathered on a hillside at midnight.

After ten minutes, when the rains hadn't come, the Seekers began to look nervous. After two hours, they began to weep. But after five hours, they were brought great news: They had spread so much light, God had changed his mind and decided to cancel the flood!

The Seekers were faced with a choice: To accept the uncomfortable truth, that they'd been wrong to sell their homes, or accept a comforting lie, that they'd saved the entire planet.

They chose the second option.

As soon as the sun came up, they launched a media campaign, and told their tale to anyone who would listen.

***

Renee also had to choose between an uncomfortable truth and a comforting lie…

It was the middle of the night.

She shook her legs, rubbed her forehead, sniffed, choked, and lifted herself up to the vent.

She caught sight of the fragment of kettle, which stopped her in her tracks:

"No, Renee, no! I need to keep a clear head. I can build on yesterday. I can become a better me."

She activated I-Green:

"*Good morning, Renee Ann. It's going to be one-of-a-kind.*"

Renee tapped her lip:

"Yesterday was one-of-a-kind. I had some sort of, how do I put this, 'Revelation'. I became aware of something new."

"*I know everything worth knowing.*"

"But what do I know?"

"*Grass is blue.*"

"Of course."

"*I'm perfect.*"

"I am? Yes... No... Hang on... Tell me something else."

"*I haven't had cheese on toast in years.*"

"Yes! That's it! I haven't had cheese on toast in years."

Her revelations began to resurface, one after the other, like drips from a leaky tap:

"I haven't achieved anything."

Drip.

"*I'm breaking my own rule.*"

Drop.

"I must have been unhappy."

Drip.

"*I must work harder.*"

"The market will only help me if I help myself."

"*I will find work!*"

"I will! But... Hang on... What if I don't?"

"*What if my knees buckle?*"

"What if my mattress is stolen?"

"*Does it matter?*"

"Does anything matter?"

"*Why am I even alive?*"

Renee bolted upright:

"I need to find out! I need to know!"

She dressed in a hurry, smeared rouge across her face, forgot to open her accessories, skipped breakfast, and stuck some gum inside her gas mask, to stop the supply of antidepressants.

She was ready to face the day.

***

It was still dark when Renee crawled outside.

A column of smoke, or perhaps it was mist, imbued the air with whimsical wonder. A lone star anticipated an operatic twilight. The floor felt soft and creamy.

"*The Muslims are coming to get me!*"

"Bloody heathens!"

"*Lock the flipping hatch!!!*"

Renee locked the hatch, stepped into the lift, and stepped out into Podsville.

She was overcome by doubt:

"Did I really lock my hatch? I recall locking it. But I locked it yesterday. Maybe that's what I remember. Maybe. Yes! I need to go back and check."

She turned, waited for the lift, and stepped inside. Five pence was added to her debt.

When she reached her pod, she was surprised to discover that two of her avatars had beaten her to it. I-Special and I-Extra were fighting, trying to check the locks, but failing to make physical contact. They collapsed in a ball, wearing harried looks, with grey eyes and frazzled hair.

Renee stumbled forwards, unlocked each lock, relocked each lock, sighed and returned to the lift.

She stumbled through Podsville, holding the walls and dragging her feet. She yawned. I-Green wobbled. I-Original fell over and began to crawl. I-Special puffed its chest:

"*I'm the only I, better than all I-Others. I shall be happy. Oh me in heaven above!*"

Renee paid it no attention.

Lightheaded and dizzy, she squatted down, and noticed a rash which covered her palm:

"What if it spreads? What if it covers my body? What if I can't make it to work? What happened to my appetite? Why does my mouth feel so dry? Oh, why am I worrying so much?"

She almost tripped over the dead cat.

The cat's skin had ruptured, collapsed and was starting to decay. It looked smaller. *Everything* looked smaller or larger, brighter or dimmer than before.

The uneven paving slab looked like a cliff edge. The Nestle Tower looked like a tiny figurine. The walls felt soft and squidgy.

The masturbating avatar seemed to shout: "Rah... Rah... Renee".
The West End Industrial Estate didn't make a sound.

It made Renee want to scream:

"Noooo!!!"

"*No! I need to be strong.*"

"*Stay strong, Renee, stay strong.*"

£113,542.16

£113,542.17

She had arrived in Oxford Circus.

***

Renee was assessed by the Podsicle Interviewer.

Un-medicated, she found the experience vaguely familiar. She recalled the way that avatar quoted figures, and the way it paid such fastidious attention to her diet. The fine details eluded her, but she didn't seem to care. She was awarded a job, hobbled through town, and arrived in front of Mansion House; a brown and white building, twenty metres wide, which was once the headquarters of the North Eastern Railway Company.

She followed her avatars inside, where she wandered between seven bedrooms, a roof terrace, wine cellar, swimming pool and sauna. She gazed on in wonderment at the bright white chandeliers, handcrafted skylights and spangly mosaics. She followed the patterns which caressed every door and panel.

Her avatars repeated the oligarch's instructions:

"*Tear it down!*"

"*Destroy it!*"

"*Fumigate the air.*"

"*Sterilize the earth.*"

"*Obliterate every atom.*"

"*Build it up.*"

"*Tear it down.*"

"*Build it up.*"

"*Tear it down.*"

"*Repeat. Repeat. Repeat.*"

She grabbed a cricket bat and smashed the windows.

Glass fell like diamond rain.

Renee paused:

"Is this… Right?… Okay?… Productive?"

"*All work is productive.*"

"*Idleness is sin.*"

"*Working ten percent faster could put me top of the Intensity Chart.*"

These words focussed Renee's mind.

She dragged a ruby-encrusted sofa over to the broken window, heaved it up and tipped it out. Her endorphins surged. She grabbed a Fabergé egg and threw it against a wall. She felt euphoric. She smashed a coffee table. She felt divine. She jumped up and down on a satin settee. She made it into the top two hundred of the London Workers' Chart.

I-Green displayed a flashing arrow, which led her to a portrait.

She viewed every carving on its hand-gilded frame, but couldn't see the painting itself. Her Plenses had converted it into an image of Renee:

"How jolly delightful!"

"*I'm delightful. Yippee!*"

Renee shivered with déjà vu.

As she tore the painting down, some plaster tumbled from the wall.

Her déjà vu grew stronger.

She smashed a Chinese dragon and nodding figurine.

Her déjà vu grew to epic proportions.

She spotted a piano, which began to morph. Its legs curved inwards, its surfaces turned gold, and monochrome designs appeared on its sides.

Renee blinked. The piano turned black.

Renee blinked. The piano turned gold.

Black. Gold. Black. Gold. Black.

Renee shuddered:

"What is this? Where have I viewed it before? Why am I viewing it now?"

She viewed a mythical beast, whose reptilian neck swished in a manner which was both speedy and slow. She viewed a lavish red carpet, a thousand chandeliers and a secret door:

"I've seen these things before. Yes! But… But where?… Perhaps… No… Perhaps… The *Night of the Broken Kettle*."

Renee's thoughts began to resurface:

"Podsicle Palace!"

"How could any I-Other afford such a palace? How could it work for two million years?"

"And my debt!"

"I earn less than I spend. I can't make a single repayment. I'll never repay my debt, I'll never retire, I'll never be… Be… Oh, it's useless."

Already suffering from overexertion, anxiety, a lack of food and a lack of sleep; these thoughts forced Renee to her knees. She pressed her head against the floor and gripped hold of the carpet.

Her avatars collapsed:

"*Give me an 'R'. Give me an 'E'. Give me a 'Nee'.*"

"*What have I got?*

"*Renee!*"

"*Go Renee, go Renee, go!*"

Renee crawled behind I-Green, stood up, and raised a Ming Dynasty vase above her head:

"No! No way! I don't want to break this. I want cheese on toast. I want Podsicle Palace. I want to keep this beautiful tub!"

Her Hesitation Ranking fell by three million places, and she fell below Paul Podell in the Compliancy Chart:

"Oh Renee. Oh me!"

She turned icy cold, felt her heart beat inside her throat, and lost her peripheral vision. She focussed on the vase, lifted it as high as she could, jumped, and brought it crashing down.

Her Compliancy Ranking climbed five places.

She panted, composed herself, and followed I-Green to a pair of candlesticks.

Her doubts resurfaced:

"Why am I smashing this? It makes no sense to break it, only to fix it again straight after. Wouldn't it be better if I did nothing at all?"

She panted:

"No! Idleness is a sin."

She paused:

"But is it?"

Under pressure from her screen, which was displaying her lowly position in several charts, Renee suppressed her doubts, picked up a chainsaw, turned it on and began to destroy the staircase; removing one baluster, nailing it back into position, removing it again, and replacing it again. She repeated this process a hundred times, moved up a step and began afresh:

"I need to do this to repay my debt. Yes! I really do need to do this! I do. I really do!"

"*Hard work is virtuous.*"

"*I'm virtuous.*"

"*I'm divine!*"

***

Renee inspected the scene. The staircase was ratty, misshapen and splintered, but it still maintained the general form of a staircase. On any other day, this would've filled our Renee with pride.

Not today:

"It's such a mess... It... It was so much better before."

She frowned:

"I need to work to repay my debt. But I'll never repay my debt. So I don't need to work. And this work doesn't need to be done. So why bother? Why bother at all?"

She paused, tried to console herself, but couldn't escape her doubts:

"The value of the things I produce is supposed to be equal to the value of the things I consume. That's simple, free-market justice. But I've never produced anything, so I've never earned the right to consume. Oh me... I haven't taken personal responsibility... What have I done?... What have I done with my life?"

She pulled her hair:

"Machines produce everything I need, whether I work or not. If anything, I'm getting in their way. So why bother? Why work? Who am I working for? Who benefits from my work? Oh Renee… I don't understand a thing."

She screamed:

"What am I going on about? I work for me! I benefit myself! Me, myself and I!"

She raised her hands and smiled:

"Oh, wonderful me! These thoughts are truly unique. No I-Other has ever had thoughts like these."

She cringed:

"But I can't *not* work. Individuals have to work! Individuals have to work individual jobs, in individual ways, but can't be so individual as to not work at all. All individuality must conform!"

Renee sucked down hard, forgetting she'd covered the nozzle in her gas mask with gum.

She choked. Her blood pressure increased, her heart palpitated and her hands became numb. But she felt compelled to push on and complete the job she'd started:

"Personal responsibility!"

"Hard work is next to me-lee-ness."

"Go Renee!"

"Go me!"

She followed I-Green to a pocket-watch, but lacked the strength to pick it up. Her limbs felt heavy, her mind clouded over, and she became acutely aware of the effort behind every breath she took.

She scrunched her eyes, grabbed the watch at the second attempt, and threw it down the stairs.

It bobbled, lethargically, as if embarrassed to be falling, and landed without incurring so much as a scratch.

She approached a diamond ring, raised her hand and collapsed.

"Everything will be alright."

"No, it won't!"

Renee was ashamed of herself for shouting at I-Green.

"I'm pathetic," she thought. "With these tender emotions, worries and doubts."

Then she snapped:

"I-Original is even worse than me! Just look at I, with my tiny little legs. I couldn't even lift a ring!"

Stuck between thoughts and words, she was unable to continue.

The Podsicle Supervisor materialised above her:

"Renee Ann Blanca. Worker 2060-5446. Aged twenty-four. Debt: £113,544.84. Available calories: Seventy-six."

Renee opened her eyes.

"In the name of the market! Renee's actions have been a crime against personal responsibility. Renee will be docked twenty million places in the London Workers' Chart and fined ten thousand pounds. Repeat performances could result in the repossession of Renee's pod and the disconnection of Renee's gas. For the good of I!"

"For the good of I."

"I, I, I."

"Me, me, me... Yes, me! What's it to accuse *me*? This thing in front of me, telling me what to do, is nothing more than light and air. It's never done a hard day's work in its life. What gives it the right to boss me? To judge me? I demand an explanation. I demand justice. I demand... I demand... I demand less indifference. It's driving me crazy. Away! Away with it! My debt won't be increased. My rankings won't be low. I'm the best, better than all I-Others. The best, I tell it, the best!"

Renee's debt increased by twenty pence for every word she spoke. At first, this caused her to worry. But Renee was filled with so many various emotions, so many doubts and fears, that these feelings soon dissolved, and merged; forming a single, amorphous ball of anxiety and shame.

She ignored the Podsicle Supervisor.

"I can't reverse my decision. My data supports my analysis.

"It would be an honour and a privilege to give Renee some advice: Be true to Renee! Think about Renee! Don't shirk, work, and Renee will never be fined again."

Renee was overcome by a tsunami of intense terror.

Her body went into *Fight or Flight* mode, producing so much adrenaline that her heartbeat became sporadic; palpitating in short bursts, discharging three quick beats, pausing, pounding, stopping and starting. Her muscles tensed, pinning her to the floor. Her mind raced from one source of anxiety to another:

"My debt! My pod! My body! My work! My debt! My arms! My rankings! My future! My pod! My fingers! My work! My heart! My debt! My gas! My I-Friends! My clothes! My jobs! My life! My work!"

Nothing seemed real. Nothing made sense.

Renee's heart went into overdrive, firing off beats like an automated gun. Her body shook her from the inside out. Her eyes bulged. Her ears rang. She began to tremble, sweat, choke and ache:

"My pod! My breaths! My debt! My rankings! My ears! My gas! My gum!"

Renee paused:

"My gum! Yes, my gum! My beautiful, beautiful gum."

Her heart crashed against her ribs.

She raised her hand a few centimetres, but lacked the strength to move it any further.

She tried again, managed to touch her face, but couldn't remove her mask.

She closed her eyes, summoned all the strength she had, raised her hand, lifted her mask, removed the gum and inhaled.

She consumed far less gas than on the *Night of the Broken Kettle*, but it had a similar effect. Her muscles relaxed, twitched, and then relaxed. Her hands tingled. Her tongue tasted of sugar. She felt light, empty, happy and free.

Her eyelids closed with skittery motion.

Everything was solid black.

Everything was silent.

Everything was still.

LOOK. SPEAK. RUN.

"Question everything."
GEORGE CARLIN

You may have heard of the Greek intellectual, Archimedes.

Legend has it that Archimedes was once set a task: To calculate the volume of a king's crown. It proved somewhat of a challenge, until Archimedes visited his local spa. Whilst scrubbing himself clean, luxuriating in those soothing waters, he saw a man step into the bath. As that man ducked below the surface, he displaced a quantity of water that had the exact same volume as his body.

"Eureka!" cried Archimedes. "Eureka! I've got it!"

Still naked, he ran outside, sprinted down the street and made his way to see the king.

"Eureka!" he cheered. "Eureka, eureka, eureka!"

***

Renee had her own *Eureka Moment*.

She awoke, groggy and lightly drugged, to find herself spread eagle across a Persian rug. Her brain pulsated and her good cheek twitched, turning from purple to plum to mauve.

She noticed her rankings, which had plummeted, and her debt, which had increased by tens of thousands of pounds. Then she noticed her avatars. I-Green looked pale and thin. I-Original was sucking its thumb. I-Extra was tearing its hair:

"*My overdraft limit has been reached.*"

"*The Bank of China won't authorize any further purchases.*"

"*My gas supply will be stopped henceforth.*"

Renee's gas mask whimpered. Then it ran dry.

She remembered her previous thoughts:

"I'll never repay my debt. I'll never retire. This life just goes on and on forever."

She shivered:

"I've never produced anything of value, so I've never earned the right to consume."

She shook:

"Machines produce everything I need. If anything, I'm getting in their way. So why bother? Why work? Who am I working for? Who benefits from my work?"

She contemplated every sound:

"*Who* am I working for?"

"*Who* benefits from my work?"

Her original response had been so emphatic:

"I work for me! I benefit myself! Me, myself and I!"

But now she wasn't so sure:

"What's this 'Who'?"

She spoke out loud:

"'Who'? But… Well… What on earth is this 'Who'?"

"*The Who were a rock and roll band from Shepherds Bush.*"

"*I'm a pinball wizard.*"

"*I'm the best.*"

"No… No, no, no… Where have I listened to that word before? Hmm… 'Who'… Did one of my avatars say it? No. Was it on Twitter? No. In town? Maybe. No, that's not it. On the… Yes! That's it! I'm sure it is. I've worked it out. I'm a blimming genius!"

Renee had remembered a photograph from her youth, which she'd discarded when she turned seven. She could just about recall the inscription on its frame:

Always be who I am.

"Who!"

That picture, which she'd seen without her Plenses, was beginning to take shape. Trees were appearing in the background. And there, front and centre, was a woman. Not Renee. Someone else.

"Mum?" Renee whispered. The very sound of that word scared her. She didn't know what it meant, or where it'd come from, but she simply couldn't ignore it.

It sounded like the whispering wind:

"Mum." Whoosh. "Mum." Hiss. "Mum."

Her eyes bulged:

"Yes! I've worked it out! 'Who' means another it, just like that figure. Real, living, breathing I-Others. Other Renees. Other mees!"

Now, beloved friend, you may deem such a statement to be rather, how should I put this, "Dull"? "Prosaic"? "Obvious"? But to Renee, these words were beyond unthinkable. They were heresy. She'd acknowledged that other people could exist! Not just as avatars, as competing workers, or rankings in a corporate chart; but as bonafide, sentient beings, not unlike herself.

It terrified her. Her heart skipped several beats. But she'd done it. She couldn't deny it. The reality of the situation had hit her between the eyes.

"Who am I working for?"

"Who benefits from my work?"

These questions showed a concern for other people. Renee wanted her work to help someone else! But why? It didn't make any sense:

"And what if it's not just work? What if I created my avatars and I-Friends because, deep down, I wanted to be friends with I-Others? *Real* I-Others? What if my selfies were an attempt to impress another me? Not an I-Friend, but a living, breathing me. What if I created I-Sex because I wanted to have sex with another me? Or touch another me? Or hold another me?"

It dawned on her:

"My successes feel hollow, because I don't have another me to enjoy them with. I need another me! I need another me!!!"

She jumped up, indifferent to the pain, performed a star-jump and screamed "Eureka!":

"That's it! I want another me. Eureka! I don't just want to own myself, I want to own another self. Eureka! Not to be alone, but... I don't know. I don't know how to say it, it's insane, but I must have it. Another self! Yes. Eureka! I can satisfy my physical needs, but not my emotional ones. I need another me. I need I-Others. Eureka! Eureka! Eureka!"

"There's no such thing as I-Others."

"I only need myself."

"Me, myself and I."

Renee wanted to disagree. But her avatars were only saying the things she'd always believed herself. They had to be right!

She shook her head and sighed:

"Oh, I've really screwed things up this time. How could I be so unprofessional? How could I question my boss? Ten thousand pounds! A million positions! What was I thinking? If only I'd worked harder. I'm such a damn fool."

She hugged her knees:

"I'm an individual. The best of the very best! How could I possibly want an I-Other? It'd influence me. It'd stop me from being me. No! I can't allow that to happen."

She covered her eyes:

"I'm a wretch. I'm not good enough. I'm useless. I've failed."

She shuddered:

"True individuals don't need I-Others. True individuals take responsibility for themselves."

She nodded, to agree with herself, paused, and then shook her head:

"No! No, no, no! Why should *I* take personal responsibility? My problems aren't *my* fault, they've been created by the system; this dirty system, which isolates me from I-Others; placing me under pressure to work, compete and consume. This system is to blame. This system should take responsibility!"

She frowned:

"No! No, no, no! I must take personal responsibility. I must find another me. I must touch another me. Mum! I must do it myself. I must do it now!"

Her certainty mixed in with her doubt:

"I can't... I can... I'll suffer... I'll prosper... No! Yes! Yes!!! That's just it: To want to live with I-Others makes me truly unique; the most individual me that ever lived!"

And now, out loud:

"I'm the best! A true individual!"

"I'm the only I, better than all I-Others."

"All individuality must conform."

"Buy five friends, get one free."

***

Low on calories, Renee struggled to walk back home.

She focussed on each step she took, lifted her chin and stumbled forwards; looking out through her screen, and viewing the world in an entirely new way.

Here was a glass panel, split by shade and light, with a dramatic smear in one corner. Here was a paving slab, stuffed full with majestic pebbles. Here was a sparkling raindrop, a carefree ball of fluff, a billowing cable, a robot, an avatar, a man?

It was almost too much to bear. Renee scratched the inside of her pockets, grabbed her breasts, jumped, whinnied and whined:

"I am! Mum! Individual! Castle of joy. Heart of hearts. Buy five get one free."

"Buy some Coca Cola right now."

Renee's avatars were leaning into the walls, collapsing, dragging themselves along, rising, stumbling and falling. There were bags under their eyes. Their hands were covered in rashes.

Renee was embarrassed. She was sure her avatars were drawing attention. She was sure these two beady eyes were growling at her from afar. These two eyes felt like laser beams. These ones burned red. These ones seemed to scream.

"Damn I-Original. I'm giving me away!"

"I'm the best," I-Original whimpered in self-defence.

"Of course I-Others want to look at me. I'm beautiful!"

"An angel."

"A goddess."

"Divine."

Renee was about to argue, but then it struck her:

"I want I-Others to look at me! I want to look at I-Others. Not just avatars: *Actual* I-Others. Let it and it look at me. Let me look at it!"

She fixed her gaze on the being before her.

The sheer intensity of this action made Renee feel woozy. She'd never done anything like it. For sure, she'd competed with other workers, and mocked their avatars, but she'd never actually viewed them:

"Do it, Renee, just do it: Acknowledge I-Others."

The vision of that male left Renee blind.

She blinked the brightness away, composed herself, inhaled, and stared into its face.

With a stooped back and bent knees, it was incapable of standing fully erect. Its protruding eyebrows bent askew at the most illogical of angles. But its eyes? What eyes! What black holes! Its eyes had been sucked into its skull. They didn't turn, focus or adjust. They simply existed, passive, like a pair of black pearls; indifferent to the world, and indifferent to our Renee.

"Why isn't it looking at me? Look at me, me-damn-it, I'm real!"

Renee continued to stare. The male continued to ignore her.

They came ever closer, but the male didn't flinch.

Inwards and onwards, they approached one harried step at a time.

Closer and closer, their noses were about to meet. Renee winced, inhaled, and braced herself for contact. She'd never touched another human, and the thought of it both thrilled and appalled her.

The male walked straight through our Renee.

"Blast!" she cursed. "Bloody avatars, made of hollow light. It and it should grow some real skin."

Renee felt deflated. And yet she also felt great. She'd done the unthinkable: She'd acknowledged that other people could exist, and she'd tried to make eye contact. She'd broken the biggest taboo:

"I'm amazing!"

"*The best.*"

"*Gillette! The best a Renee can get.*"

Renee wanted more. Like an addict, for whom one hit was never enough, she wanted a second high, just as soon as she'd experienced the first. She wanted to make eye contact with a real human being. She wanted them to acknowledge her existence and think she was great.

She looked around and saw about fifty other beings, excluding her own avatars, but none of them were looking at her.

She screamed:

"Look at me! Acknowledge me! Don't leave me here on my own!"

She ran towards the nearest being, a teenager with the pinched-face of a geriatric. She stared into its eyes. But the teenager didn't repay the compliment. It walked straight through our Renee.

She ran across the street, leaving her own avatars in her wake. She stood before an elderly female with scattered teeth and chapped skin. It also passed through her.

Renee ran forwards, ran back, ran here, ran there, crossed the road and crossed back. She tried to make eye contact with this male with sunburned elbows, this female with droopy lashes and this child with a triangular face. She didn't engender a reaction:

"I don't want avatars. I want I-Others. Real I-Others. At least one I-Other must be real!"

She didn't give in. She took detours, visited side streets, looked into one being's eyes and then another's; hoping beyond hope that they'd acknowledge, see or touch her.

Building up a resistance to her drug of choice, each new attempt gave Renee a little less satisfaction.

She screamed:

"I can't be alone anymore. I need to be acknowledged. I need another me."

"I'd be happier if I-Others didn't exist."

"I-Others are the worst."

"No, no, no! I'm wrong. Shut up. I'm all wrong!"

Renee's avatars didn't know how to react. They searched for data which didn't exist and ran algorithms which had no end. Renee's hairclip began to steam. I-Special turned grey with static, I-Original lost its features, I-Green crashed and I-Extra disappeared.

Renee pushed ahead.

Compelled by a certain sense of stubbornness, she made eye contact with every being she passed. Now with this raw-boned female. Now with this stocky male. She gazed pleadingly at this youngster with curved lips. She glared intensely at this child with oversized hands.

They all walked through her.

Renee debriefed:

"I've acknowledged I-Others. That's courageous. I've walked towards several its. That's big. I've tried to make eye contact. Holy me! But it and it haven't reacted. I need to do more. I need to be noticed."

A middle-aged female approached Renee as she passed beneath the Nestle Tower. Its face took the shape of a ship's bow. It had stooped shoulders and ruddy skin.

Renee looked into its eyes and said "Hello".

Indifferent to her debt, which had risen by twenty pence, she was pleased with her own audacity. Although, it must be said, she was surprised to discover she wasn't *more* pleased. What she'd done was revolutionary. She'd spoken to another being! Of course, she'd hurled abuse at the air, when prompted by I-Special, but she'd never looked into another being's eyes, acknowledged their existence and offered up a benevolent word. No one had. Her actions had diverged from the very laws of nature.

"Hello there," she continued in a nervous hush. "Hello, I'm Renee."

A pound was added to her debt.

Her eyes pleaded for a response, she frowned with desperation, but the female didn't flinch.

"What a fool!" Renee screamed. "Is it deaf or just ignorant? I was trying to be nice!"

I-Original managed to whimper:

"I-Others are scum."

I-Special flickered and flashed.

Renee took a deep breath:

"Perseverance is next to me-liness. I will push on!"

She ran up to a punk with purple hair:

"Hello".

She ran up to a hippy with painted nails:

"I'm the best".

She ran up to a skater with gaudy tattoos:

"I want to be friends".

The punk walked through her, the hippy crossed the road and the skater turned down an alley.

She ran up to this grey-haired reactionary, this dreadlocked Rastafarian and this puffed-up child. She said "Hello", "Let's talk", "Let's unite", "Respect me" and "Be courageous".

No one reacted.

She ran up to this purple-haired pensioner, this clean-shaven giant and this pimply adolescent. She said "Hi", "Let's chat", "I exist", "Acknowledge me" and "Respond".

No one seemed to care.

I-Original's heartbeat became sporadic; palpitating in short bursts, discharging three quick beats, pausing, pounding, stopping and starting. Its muscles tensed, pinning it to the floor. Its eyes bulged.

Renee didn't care.

Her debt shot upwards.

She didn't care.

She'd experienced the sweet high of rebellion, and she wanted another hit.

She approached this freckled youngster with tightly-drawn hair, this male with a wart on its nose and this stout-faced old female.

They didn't react.

She turned into Podsville.

She said "View me", "Listen to me", "Touch me" and "Feel me".

She didn't receive a reply.

She might have continued forever, but she'd arrived outside her pod. She shook her head, wheezed, unlocked the hatch, crawled inside, gobbled down some calorie-substitute, downed a protein shake, rocked a little, was overcome by exhaustion, closed her eyes and fell asleep.

TURN RIGHT AT
THE LIGHTS

"Vision is the art of seeing
what's invisible to others."
JONATHAN SWIFT

Once upon a time there lived a lion cub, whose mother died shortly after she was born. She wandered, aimless and alone, until she found a herd of sheep. Most of them ran away. But one brave soul took pity on the young lion, waved it over and raised it as her own.

The lion cub learned from her adopted mother. She began to eat grass and bleat like a real sheep. She was happy, but she wasn't content. She felt her life was missing some sort of vital ingredient.

One day, at the dawn of spring, her herd stopped by a riverbank to drink. The young lion leaned down, saw her reflection in the water, panicked, and let out a devilish roar. It was so loud, and so fearsome, that it scared all her companions away.

***

Renee screamed:

"Aaaargh!!!"

She'd awoken in a state of hope and fear.

She'd remembered her revelations, and how she'd tried to engage with other people. This had filled her with hope. She believed she was standing on the precipice of greatness.

Then she'd remembered her debt, rankings and credit rating. This had filled her with fear. She couldn't afford the very necessities she needed to survive.

She opened Alexa and ordered a tube of calorie-substitute.

Seventeen red letters flashed up on her pod's main screen:

INSUFFICIENT CREDIT

She tried again and received the same message. She ordered a lab-built apple, which only cost eighty pence, but those letters continued to flash. She tried to buy the cheapest item she could find, an imitation crabstick, but was unable to make the purchase.

Those lights reverberated through Renee's mind: Red. White. Red. White. Red.

She closed her eyes, inhaled, opened her eyes and checked her food: About fifty grams of carbohydrate powder, two strips of genetically modified salmon jerky, a portion of pre-cooked artificial rice and the remains of some calorie-substitute:

"I need to work, to earn money, so I can afford to buy more food. But I can't. I just can't do it! Enough of this treadmill life. Enough of this recurring nightmare of humdrum days and pointless jobs. My work isn't productive. It doesn't help me. It doesn't help I-Others. It just - doesn't - help."

Her exacerbation was making Renee loquacious:

"Don't I want to be free? Don't I understand freedom? I'm a slave! I've imprisoned myself and need to escape."

She dressed, smeared foundation across her cheek, stopped herself, and threw the tin of foundation away. She took her makeup bag, turned it upside-down, and brushed the debris aside. She grabbed her hairclip, bent it out of shape, and watched her screen disappear:

"Goodbye false prophets. Goodbye fake friends. Goodbyes unreality. Hello world!"

She lay back down:

"I've been allowed to do whatever work I've chosen, so long as I've worked. I've been allowed to consume anything I've wanted, so long as I've consumed. I've been winning the battles but losing the war. Enough is enough! I don't want a meaningless job. I don't want to consume for consumption's sake. I want to be free. I want to leave!"

Renee sat up with a swagger, enchanted by the intoxicating awareness of her own true self:

"I-Others don't refuse to work! I-Others don't leave! I'm going to do it. I'll be a real individual. I'll – win – life!"

She took her spare shirt, tied it in knots and filled it with food.

She used her spare trousers to tie that pack around her shoulders. She put her hairclip in her pocket, as a keepsake, grabbed her gas mask and left without locking the hatch.

***

As soon as she stepped out from the lift, Renee spotted a septuagenarian. It was beige, long-faced and milky-eyed, with bitten lips and an oversized Adam's apple. Its attempts to hold itself upright suggested a steely sort of determination. Its crooked back suggested its life had been hard.

Renee made eye contact and said "Hello".

The septuagenarian ignored her.

Renee was about to react, but stopped short when she realised *she* might be to blame.

It was a radical thought:

"There's something missing. But what… It's… I mean… Hang on a darn-totting minute. I don't even know if it's real! If it's an avatar, I shouldn't waste my breath. But is it? Is it real? Avatar or… I need to know. I need to find out!"

Renee inhaled, lifted her finger to her eye and removed a Plense. Rather than *view* the world through that filter, she *saw* it for what it really was.

She saw a rat, which scurried between her legs.

She shuddered. Renee had never encountered a rat before, and the very sight of its sinuous tail filled her with fright. Moved by a primeval instinct for self-preservation, her heart jumped, *she* jumped, and wisps of her hair stood on end.

She closed her eyes, trembled, focussed on her breathing, counted to ten, and slowly lifted her eyelids.

It took her several moments to acknowledge the scene. Everywhere she'd viewed an avatar, she now saw a rat.

Occasionally, her one remaining Plense would convert those rats into avatars; making them look like real human beings. Then her Plenseless eye would reveal their murine form.

Rat. Avatar. Rat.

This barrel-stomached youth became a chubby rat with

vampirish teeth and humanoid hands. This petite brunette became a skinny rat with devilish eyes. This bald male became a hairless rat. This female became a fluffy one.

Rat. Avatar. Rat.

Renee blinked as quickly as she could:

"That explains why no I-Others responded when I said 'Hello'. But… Hang on… What happened to all the I-Others? Did it and it die? Did it and it even exist? Have I always been alone? What have I been competing with in my charts? I need I-Others. I need another me!"

She took a deep breath, warbled, and removed her second Plense.

A curtain was raised, and Renee's street revealed itself in all its mucky glory. She wasn't in a narrow alley, between two walls of pods, as she'd always believed. The stack of pods behind her was only fifteen units high. The top of a second stack was just about visible in the distance. Between these two blocks, a giant rubbish heap filled the street. It stopped a metre short of Renee's pod, forming the so-called "Alley" down which she'd always walked.

Buried in the debris, were the pieces of kettle Renee had thrown from her pod. Here were some discarded wrappers, empty tubs and shattered bottles. Here were some cracked screens and torn mattresses; some rotting flesh, which would soon disappear, and some plastic, which would remain in place forever. A gluey mixture of urine and faeces was holding it all in place.

The smell! It was as if her eyes were sending a message to Renee's nose:

"Sweet, glorious me!"

Here was the smell of rotting fish, bad breath and wet dog. Here was the smell of a thousand dead rats. This smell was eggy, with a tinge of toxic sweetness. This smell was moist, with overtones of moss.

Renee gagged. The rank odour of that place had entered her mouth. She could taste the manure and mildew. She could feel the sewage drip down into her lungs.

She closed the food-tube on her gas mask and tried to ignore the stench.

***

Renee took slow, ponderous steps. Without a screen to display her debt, she felt no need to make bounding strides. Without her avatars to guide her, she had to stare at the ground; picking her way around this puddle of ooze, this mouldy apple and this empty bottle.

Renee turned left out of Podsville and almost tripped over the dead cat. She couldn't believe what she saw. Here was a maggot-infested stomach, exposed to the sky. Here were two rotting legs. But this was no cat. This was a man! He had reddened bones and a strong, twisted nose. His eye-sockets were empty and his skin looked like overcooked pork.

"I'm not alone!" Renee cheered. "I've finally found another me."

Her ears turned purple. She performed a star-jump and punched the air:

"I *am* alone. All alone! Oh, so alone."

She kicked the corpse, and berated it with absolute malevolence:

"How dare it be dead! How dare it! Think of me. I need it. Oh Renee. Oh me."

It dawned on her:

"I-Original! Oh, how could I curse I? I wasn't trying to trip me, I was helping me to clear the path."

She inhaled hard, instinctively, forgetting her gas had been disconnected. She steadied herself, and continued through Russell Square.

This part of town seemed much the same as before. Glassy green towers still shot up like giant prison bars, reaching the sky, which was still a roof of grey. But the streets were now strewn with litter, several windowpanes were missing or smashed, and rats now scurried where avatars once wandered. Renee didn't see a single person until she turned a corner and caught sight of the masturbating man.

He was dressed as normal, in brown corduroy trousers, tied up with string, and shoes which were covered in scratches. But something seemed slightly off.

Renee stopped to stare. Coming face to face with another living person, for the first time in her life, had rendered her numb. She covered her eyes, uncovered them, and finally accepted the truth.

I-Special had been wrong. This man didn't have a cherubic, shiny face. Life had worn him down, sandpapering his skin and chiselling his cheeks. He was shrunken, shrivelled, frail, grey and old. His lips were glued together with dried saliva. He had a star-shaped birthmark on his lower lip.

There was something else…

This man's hand was indeed jerking up and down, but it wasn't inside his pants. He wasn't masturbating. He was holding up his palm, which was trembling with weakness. By his feet stood a cardboard sign:

Homeless and hungry. Please spare some food.

Renee scratched her head:

"Why would I spare some food? I eat food. It might rot if I spared it."

She stared at the man as he tried to open his mouth.

After several minutes, a small gap appeared at the side of his mouth. This gap began to spread, unzipping his lips a millimetre at a time.

His eyes were desperate. Renee couldn't overcome the feeling that he wasn't so much staring *at* her, but staring *into* her; penetrating every atom of her being.

She clutched her bag:

"It can sense my discomfort. I must look frozen stiff. Oh, what if it rejects me? What if I put it out? I don't want to disturb it. I don't want to be a nag."

She wanted to approach that man. Indeed, this had been her plan all along: To approach the first person she found, look into their eyes and say "Hello". But here, in the real world, things weren't nearly so simple.

Her muscles tensed.

She was terrified the man might reply, and she wouldn't know what to do. She was terrified he might *not* reply, and ignore her very existence. She opened her mouth to speak, but was unable to make a sound.

Her body refused to turn her thoughts into actions.

She became overwhelmingly conscious of herself. She thought her legs were too straight, and so she bent her knees. She shook her feet, which made her feel ridiculous, and so she puffed her chest to compensate. She felt she'd gone too far, and so she looked back down at her feet.

The wind seemed to whisper her name: "Rah... Rah... Renee?"

It was all too much to bear.

She pivoted and sprinted away, without paying attention to where she was heading. Instead of turning left, towards Oxford Circus, she turned right, crossed the Euston Road, passed through Camden and continued up the Highgate Road.

***

The rats and litter subsided.

The sky seemed brighter.

Everything was black or green...

Industrial towers gave way to derelict buildings; ancient, abandoned and ashen. Houses dripped with solid dust. Shop windows contained no glass. Pylons, blackened with char, looked naked without their cables.

And yet, amidst this dark malaise, Mother Nature was winning her war; reclaiming the land which had once been hers. Tendrils of ivy had commandeered Victorian townhouses. Trees had grown up through helpless homes. Grass had broken through the tarmac.

Renee focussed on that grass. She could vaguely understand that it was, in fact, grass. And yet she couldn't quite believe it.

"No," she thought. "Grass is blue. What on earth is this green stuff? I must be hallucinating. I must be insane."

She tried to blink the grass blue:

"It can't be grass. No. Perhaps it's a mutation. Or perhaps the blue layer was scrubbed away.

"And what are these? These brown poles with green hats. I've viewed these before. But where? On the... No. Hang on... Wait a minute.... Yes! On the picture. Mum! In the background were some brown poles with bushy green hats. This 'Mum' character must be close. Perhaps... Yes!... Perhaps... Perhaps it's the other me I've been looking for!"

Renee felt the sort of giddy excitement that comes naturally to us in childhood, but is usually forgotten with age; a tingly sensation, which whizzed through her arms and forced her eyes wide open.

She stopped, looked up at a tree, and caught sight of something peculiar. To you, it might look like a common robin. You might not give it a second glance. But Renee had never seen a robin. She'd never seen a bird:

"Sweet vibrations of me!"

She joined it in song:

"Cheer-up, cheerily, cheer-up, cheer-ooh."

When the robin hopped along its branch, Renee danced in a circle. When it flapped its wings, Renee flapped her arms:

"Cheer-up, cheerily, cheer-up, cheer-ooh."

The bird flew away.

Renee tried to fly. She failed, unsurprisingly, and landed with a thud:

"Oh me. Oh my. It was so... So... Joyous! I want that joy. I want to sing and dance and fly. Yes. But there was something else... Hmm... What was it? Yes! Its clothes! There wasn't a Nike swoosh in sight. It didn't have a single accessory. That must be it: Nakedness. Nakedness is joy!"

Renee tore her clothes from her body, one piece at a time. Her shirt landed on a bench, her trousers landed in a bush, and her underwear was caught by the wind, which carried it down the street.

On she went; flapping at a crow, which remained just out of reach:

"Look at me go! This is the most individual thing any it has ever done. I-Others may wear different clothes, may customise, may accessorise, but it and it all wear clothes. Not me! I'm as individual as it gets. I – win – life."

Renee gazed with wonder at every tree she passed: At this outstretched maple, which seemed to demand the sun's attention; at this oak, whose roots gripped hold of the broken tarmac; at these trees, which looked so tiny from afar; and these ones, which slouched, or stood erect, or had bark that could tell a thousand stories.

Seeing these trees made Renee feel euphoric. But seeing so many trees together, when she arrived in Hampstead Heath, was almost too much to bear. She froze, recalled the homeless man, grimaced, cursed, and looked up to find her screen.

Her fingers pressed imaginary buttons in the sky.

She closed her eyes, inhaled, and took a slow, tremulous step.

Struggling to think for herself, she waited for I-Green to make a suggestion, or for I-Extra to issue an alert.

Her eyes were drawn to a nostalgic horizon, where earth blurred into sky, and sky blurred into earth. Spots of yellow pockmarked the valley, as young daffodils tried to bloom. The heath smelled of poached pears, pollen and mulch.

A low haze cloaked the vista.

But Renee's avatars didn't appear. No I-Friend came to help. No screen offered any assistance.

Renee had no choice but to imagine I-Green for herself. And here it was, with a twinkle in its eye and a thousand sequins on its dress.

So began an imaginary conversation in Renee's mind:

"*That water looks divine.*"

"Ah yes, the water. What a grand idea."

"*I am pretty grand.*"

"I am, yes, I am!"

Renee strode through the long grass, displacing seeds and squelching the mud. She felt something brush past her ankle, jumped with fright, and then smiled with glee. She listened to some nightingales, soliloquizing in the brambles. She listened to a woodlark who was singing out of tune.

She sat down by the lake.

Its surface sparkled, as if covered by a million turquoise gems. Some lilies floated by, without ever floating away.

Renee leaned down to drink, saw her reflection in the water, panicked, and let out a devilish roar:

"Aaagh! What's this ugly beast, hiding in this pond? Get away! Get away! Be gone, foul blob of corruption."

It was the first time she had seen her face, unedited by her screens, and she couldn't believe it was her own. The sight of her plastic cheek filled her with a drunken mix of fear and loathing. Her Botox-damaged eye made her want to scream.

She shuffled backwards, away from the lake, hugged her knees, waited, waited some more, and was disappointed when the monster didn't return:

"Why doesn't it want to view me? Am I too beautiful? Am I too good?"

She took a deep breath, puffed her chest and shuffled towards the lake.

As she poked her head over the water, the monster reappeared from below. She shot back and the monster shot back. She returned and the monster returned. She moved to the side and the monster moved with her:

"It's not... It's not a monster... No... It's... It's me... But... But how? How can I look like that? I was so beautiful before. No! I want to go back. I want to be perfect again. I'm really not perfect at all."

She remembered the homeless man:

"Why couldn't I approach it? What's wrong with me? Why aren't I perfect anymore?"

She imagined her holographic screen, watched her rankings tumble, watched her debt increase, and listened to an infinity of echoic voices:

"My debt could be erased with 6500 easy repayments."

"I'd be guaranteed a job if I returned to Oxford Circus."

"I belong in Podsville."
"Podsville is safe."
"This place is scary."
"There's too much space."
"There's too much freedom."
"I need to escape from this freedom!"
She pinched her thigh:
"No, Renee, no. Don't be so frigging insane!"

In an attempt to evade these voices, she put her fingers in her ears and gazed out at the heath.

Everything she saw seemed content. These flowers bloomed, unconsciously, without any thoughts or desires. These geese took great pleasure from the breeze. There wasn't a single league table in sight. These ducks weren't competing to dive the deepest, quack the loudest, or swim the furthest. Those trees weren't attempting to monopolise the air.

Each creature was sensitive to the needs of the others. When a duck got too close to a swan, the swan looked up and the duck backed away. When the shore became congested, some geese dived in for a swim.

Renee watched two dogs sleep together, entwined, using each other as pillows. She watched two cats lick each other clean.

"What are it and it doing?" she asked the imaginary version of I-Green.

I-Green shrugged.

"Why aren't the meows like me? Why aren't I like the flappers? Why don't the quackers compete? Why don't the colour-sticks think? What fools! What damn harmony! Oh me. Oh my."

Renee sighed, smiled, and spent the next few hours observing this scene.

***

As soon as she lay down to rest, her body began to itch. She unwrapped her makeshift bag and put on her spare trousers and shirt. She chewed her salmon jerky, ate her calorie-substitute and looked out through the grass.

She watched a group of burying beetles. Working together, they carried a dead mouse to open ground, dug up the earth, dumped the mouse and took it in turns to lay their eggs on top.

Renee thought she was going mad:

"Why aren't the beasts competing? What's wrong with it and it? Any individual beast could've had the dead thing to itself."

Her mind raced:

"But am I really so different? I wanted to unite with the male with the silly sign. I wanted to be like the funny beasts."

Physically exhausted from her walk, and mentally exhausted by the things she'd seen, Renee was unable to control her thoughts:

"Why couldn't I say 'Hello' to the silly man? What's wrong with me? If the beasts can come together, why couldn't I?"

That encounter repeated itself in Renee's mind.

Here she was, fixed in position, staring at the beggar's face; that weatherworn face, which hadn't succumbed to Individutopian vanity. Here she was, trying to move, trying to say "Hello"; unable to move, unable to say "Hello"; pivoting, sprinting, escaping, failing:

"But I want another me! I need another me. I have to have another me. And I *will* have another me. I know it, I just know it. It's my mission, my goal, and I always achieve my goals. I'm Renee Ann Blanca. I'm the best!

"But what if I freeze again? What if I meet the same I-Other, and it remembers how I failed? What if I meet a new I-Other, and can't speak, or stutter, or only manage to mumble? What if I meet a group of I-Others? What if it and it stare and laugh and point? Is this what I want? Yes! I need I-Others. But can I handle it? No! I don't know. I just don't know."

Renee twisted and turned. She asked herself hundreds of different questions, came up with hundreds of different answers, but couldn't find satisfaction. Dust crept up her ankles, her hair knotted and her cuffs began to fray. She became distressed by the rushing desolation of the night sky; by the oily surface of the lake, which seemed to be alive; and by the haggard moon, which illuminated everything, without revealing anything at all.

This fearful, wild night, would've kept her awake, if only it wasn't so exhausting.

She closed her eyes and fell into a catatonic slumber.

NORTH

I'm still here, observing our Renee, but she's not as clear as before. I don't feel as though I'm with her. I'm watching her through a single lens and the view is restricted.

Like a daughter who's left home, and rarely calls, I fear we're drifting apart. My love for her is still strong, but I can't be sure if it's reciprocated.

Just look at her now! Can you see her, here, with this dirtied face and tousled hair? Have you ever seen anything like it?

My word. Growing pains are the worst!

Renee is lifting her knee to her chest. It's sore from where she's been lying, rigid, on the uneven ground. There are insects in her hair, which is matted; bent forwards and backwards in clumps. Her plastic cheek is browned and her natural cheek is grazed.

She eats the rest of her food, worries about where her next meal will come from, stands up, drinks some pond water and continues north.

***

The sight of so many abandoned homes made Renee quiver with discomfort. She could almost see the lives which had once been lived, and was overwhelmed by the sheer weight of their absence; by the walls, which looked like wrinkled skin; by the sloping roofs, which were shedding their tiles; and by the foundations, which were sinking into the ground; burying themselves, in a funeral procession which had lasted for decades.

She made a conscious decision to avoid these urban spaces whenever she could; traipsing through a series of parks and golf clubs, whilst trying to catch the same crow as the day before.

She pretended I-Green was by her side.

Together, they observed the natural world with wide-eyed wonderment, held imaginary conversations, and asked questions that neither of them could answer. They felt nature had something to teach them, but couldn't decipher its language.

They watched some birds fly by in formation, without realising that the strongest birds were taking turns to fly at the front. They watched an eagle call to its friends, unaware it was inviting them to dine on the remains of a dead horse. They watched a variety of creatures play a variety of games; chasing each other, wrestling each other, throwing up scraps and trying to catch them:

"Why are the beasts doing that?"

"It doesn't make any sense."

"Beasts are bonkers."

"Doolally mad!"

***

Copying a deer, Renee had eaten some dandelions for lunch, but this had done little to quell her hunger. She hadn't experienced any sort of advertising, didn't long for synthetic food, and was keen to discover what treats might be lurking in this strange new world.

She emerged to the north of Barnet:

"Wow!"

A vast meadow opened up before her.

The mustardy smell of rapeseed filled the air. Yellow pools of that crop still pockmarked the meadow, but it was by no means alone. Here were some grasses and herbs, which had taken root shortly after this field was abandoned. Here were some shrubs, which had arrived a few years later. And there, camouflaging a distant motorway, were a line of trees, which had sprouted after more than a decade.

"This 'Mum' character lives near the brown poles with green hats."

"It does!"

"Yes, it does."

"Yes! That's what this is about! I need to find this 'Mum'. I need to find it now!"

Renee bounded through the meadow, enthused and excited, imagining I-Green by her side. She tripped on some brambles, fell, brushed herself off and continued on her way.

When she reached the trees, she caressed their wizened bark. Then she saw it, between an oak and an elm:

"Apples! I knew there was something about the bushy poles. It and it love me. It and it are the answer!"

She performed a star-jump, smiled that goofy smile of hers, and looked up in search of her screen:

"Food, glorious food!"

"I'm probably first in the Food Finding Rankings."

"I probably am."

She paused:

"But why on earth would Nestle attach its apples to this bushy pole? It doesn't make any sense. Why not deliver it by drone? It's just so... So..."

"Unprofitable?"

"Unproductive!"

Renee shivered:

"Perhaps it's a trap. O.M.R.! Nestle want to poison me, so I have to return to London and buy medicine.

"Oh, why did I leave? Why couldn't I speak to that male? Why? Why???"

"Damn Nestle."

"Damn me."

Renee cringed, backed away and sat down by the elm.

She felt a sudden urge to pick an apple, restrained herself, thought about the homeless man, thought about the apples, tapped the elm, clicked her knuckles, grew hungrier, rose, and told herself it was a trap.

"A trap!"

"Yes, a blimming trap."

***

The sun arced across the sky at a snail's pace.

Renee believed everything was perfectly still, until a grasshopper leaped past her nose. It hopped off into the distance, fleeing in fear of its life.

"Should I flee? Am *I* under attack?"

"Attack! Attack! Let's go!"

Renee jumped up, stopped herself, and assessed the threat.

She could only find a single ant:

"What? Why? It doesn't make any sense. Why would the big bug flee from the little one?"

"It could kill it."

"It could've had the little bug for breakfast."

Renee pondered this issue for several minutes, before catching sight of a second ant, and then a third. They were congregating around the grasshopper's den.

She had the strangest thought:

"The big bug wasn't scared of the little bug. It was scared of thousands of little bugs, united together as one."

"Together it and it were strong."

"But no! It doesn't make any sense. No, no, no! What sort of place is this, where up is down and black is white? The little bugs shouldn't be working together. It and it should be competing to be the best."

A vein protruded from Renee's forehead.

She watched two ants touch antennae. One ant regurgitated some liquid, which the other ant consumed.

Even though Renee observed this whole scene, she ignored the exchange of food, and told herself the ants had been using their antennae to fight.

Another two ants united, lifted a leaf many times their size, and carried it away.

Renee assumed they both wanted the leaf for themselves, and would pull apart at any moment.

She continued to watch these ants whilst the sky began to fall, dripping phantasmagorical colours: Gold, then apricot, then red. It was vermillion by the time two rabbits jumped through the grass, found an apple, shared it and bounced away.

Renee scratched her head:

"It and it seem fine."

"Not poisoned."

"No. Absolutely A-Okay."

She stood up, ambled across to the apple tree, bent down and found an apple on the ground. Her heart pounded. She lifted the apple to her face, inspected it from every angle, moved it to her mouth and nibbled its skin:

"Sweet me on my royal throne! It's so much better than other apples. But why? Is it sweeter? Is it crunchier? It's better, for sure, but it's impossible to say why."

"*Impossible.*"

"Not possible at all."

She reached up, picked an apple from the tree, bit into it, and smiled until her cheeks began to spasm. Then she smiled some more:

"It's even better than the last one!"

She ate a third apple and then a fourth:

"I'm not rocking. But I always rock when I eat. Why aren't I rocking? Why?"

She almost panicked, realised it didn't matter, grabbed a fifth apple and then a sixth.

Bloated and satiated, she curled up into a ball and closed her eyes.

***

The sun was still resting on the horizon, when Renee was awoken by the sound of distant footsteps.

She stared through the shadows and saw two ghost-like figures approach.

The first, a woman, was as white as milk. She looked like a skeleton cloaked in Nike swooshes. Her shirt was covered in holes, torn and stained. It hung loose from her crooked shoulders. Patches of hair hung limply from her scalp.

But the man!

Renee had never come across a face stamped with so much angst and agony. He was an alpha male: Tall, strong and rugged. But the glint in his eye revealed a level of fear that betrayed his muscular form. He held his head a full ten centimetres in front of his neck, as if sniffing for danger. He whinnied and puffed like a horse, turning sharply from side to side, with his fangs exposed and his hands held ready for combat.

Oblivious to each other, and oblivious to Renee, they flapped at the crows which hovered above them; walking like zombies, with their arms outstretched; snaking right, snaking left, reaching the apple tree, circling it, and circling each other.

Renee refused to believe her eyes:

"I-Others aren't real. It and it can't have escaped. It'd mean I'm not unique. No! That just wouldn't do."

She hugged her knees:

"I exist. I know it, I just know it. But how? Because I think! I think, therefore I am. I can't believe my own eyes or ears, what I listen to or view. That male is a product of my imagination. That female is light and air. It and it don't exist, but I do. I think, therefore I am! I *am* the only one who escaped. I *am* an individual. I – win – life!"

The man bit into an apple.

"No!!!! What fresh hell is this?

"If I was imagining it, it wouldn't be able to hold that apple. Unless the apple was imaginary too. But no, I've picked an apple myself. The apple *is* real. It really is eating an apple. It's stealing *my* apple!"

Renee screamed:

"That's *my* apple! Mine, all mine! How dare it take my apple? The fiend! It's *my* apple. Give it to me. Give me my Nestle now!"

Renee lunged forwards and grabbed the apple, but the man just palmed her aside.

She landed on her shoulder, which immediately began to throb.

She wanted to make eye contact and say "Hello", but her body refused to put her thoughts into action. Her muscles tensed, she became overwhelmingly conscious of herself, and overwhelmingly conscious of the man. She worried he might reply, and she worried he might not.

She had a thought:

"Hang on a bleating minute! I *have* spoken to it. I told it 'That's my apple' and 'Give me my Nestle now'. It and I made contact when it pushed me away. I've spoken to another me! I've touched another me! I can do it. I can!"

Renee performed a star-jump. This time, however, she didn't look up in search of her screen. She didn't freeze, or stutter, or turn and run away. She didn't worry about the man's reaction. Overcome by a rush of confidence, she approached the man, put her hand on his shoulder and spoke in a bombastic tone:

"Hello! I'm Renee. I'm superb."

The man shoved Renee aside, turned his head, grunted, and ate another apple.

Renee approached the woman.

"Hello," she said. "I exist! I was in the top ten of the Head Scratching Chart."

The woman didn't react.

Renee turned to the man and said "Hello". She turned to the woman and said "Hello". Man. Woman. Man.

They didn't react.

"It's not enough."

"*I need to do more.*"

"I need them to acknowledge my existence."

"*I need them to respond.*"

She ran here, ran there, said "Acknowledge me", said "I'm the best", tapped the woman and pinched the man.

She paused, put her finger on her lower lip, and realised her companions weren't wearing their gas masks. She tried to make eye contact, persevered when they flinched, pointed to their faces, pointed to *her* face, removed her gas mask, panicked, almost replaced it, composed herself, placed her gas mask on the ground and gave a thumbs-up.

The air was delicious. Far from civilisation, it had cleansed itself and returned to its natural state.

"There!" she said to the woman. "Look at me now. I look just like it!"

The woman looked up.

Renee spotted something in her face. Something minor: A twitch, or perhaps a softening.

Renee wanted more:

"But it's probably wearing its Plenses. What else can I expect?"

She smiled, softly, backed away, and addressed the woman from afar:

"It and I can talk in the morning. I mean... I couldn't speak to I-Others at first... It's hard. I understand. It needs time. In the morning... It and I will speak in the morning."

The woman didn't react.

Renee shrugged, sighed, and settled beneath a tree.

From her lowly position, she gazed up at the birds on the uppermost branches. They were protecting the smaller birds beneath them, flapping their wings whenever an intruder approached.

Renee looked out at the man, and then at the women. She checked they were there, and she checked they were real. She wondered if they would protect *her* if an intruder approached.

A house sparrow returned and shared its food.

Together, those birds created a symphony of sound. It was almost too much to bear. But the more she listened, the more Renee's ears adjusted. She noticed the melodies, then the rhythms, then the sheer joy which welded that choir together.

It rocked our Renee to sleep.

***

She didn't sleep for long.

She was awoken by the sound of heavy panting. She could smell the warm, moist, meaty breath which was saturating the air. She could feel the paw prints which were tickling the ground.

Eight pairs of demonic eyes were glowing like rubies in the darkness.

Renee was surrounded by wolves.

They were huge.

When the human population was herded into London, most household pets had died; locked inside, without access to food or the ability to fend for themselves. But some dogs had escaped. Some had interbred with wolves, producing intelligent packs of wolf-dogs, which prowled the prairies at night.

Renee could see them now. She could see their psychotic scowls, corrupted eyes, open jaws, sharp teeth, spread legs and horizontal ears.

Her heart began to thud:

Bah-boom. Pause. *Bah-boom.* Pause. *Bah-boom.*

She sat up, quivered, and tried to assess the scene:

"I should've never left home."

"Podsville was bad, but at least it was safe."

"What should I do?"

"Survive!"

"Well, duh!"

Renee tutted, rolled her eyes and searched for her companions.

The man was stood beneath a tree. His fangs were exposed, his hands were outspread and his jacket was flapping like a cape.

He kicked some stones as he hollered:

"A-woo-gah! A-woo-gah! Be gone! I'm the strongest me on the planet: The best of the very best. I'll eat every monster alive."

Renee was startled by the man's voice. He continued to puff like a horse, which added an echo to each word he spoke, but his pitch betrayed him. He sounded like a choirboy who'd inhaled too much helium:

"Aaargh! Let's be having you. Bring it on! I'm twelfth in the Aggression Rankings. I'm top of the Monster Killing Chart!"

Renee tried hard not to giggle.

The wolves closed in.

Renee tried hard not to pee her pants. She curled up into a ball and did her best to remain silent.

Out of the corner of her eye, she caught a glimpse the woman, illuminated by the orange moon. The woman's head jolted towards the man, and then back towards the wolves. She took sharp, short, heavy breaths.

Overcome by fear, concerned only with her own survival, she pivoted and sprinted away; leaving her companions to deal with the wolves.

But the wolves were hardwired to chase their prey. They leaped into action; pouncing on the woman and sinking their teeth into her neck, which snapped without resistance.

Renee almost screamed.

Two crows cawed.

The third crow flew away.

Blood squirted from the woman's throat, glistened in the moonlight, and fell like crimson rain. The woman's legs gave way. Her torso dropped like a stone.

The wolves tore flesh from bone.

Renee trembled:

"What are the furry beasts doing? If it and it want to eat, it should order some food from Amazon. There's no need to be so mean."

She didn't know how to react. The sheer majesty of the attack had thrilled her. The fountain of blood had filled her with whimsy. But the sight of the woman's head, hanging limply from her shoulders, had frightened our Renee immensely. Her chest tightened and she struggled to breathe:

"That could've been me. What if I'm next? Why are I-Others like that? Why???"

She couldn't help but stare:

"Why eat another me? Why not eat some meat? It doesn't make any sense."

Her lips felt dry:

"Furry beasts are faster than me, with sharper teeth and nails. It and it can play this game alone. So why do it together? Why split the meal? Why???"

She trembled, squeezed her knees, held an imaginary conversation with I-Green, worried, panicked and waited.

She had no idea how long it took the wolves to finish their meal. It could've been seconds, minutes or hours. But the wolves did eventually finish, and Renee did eventually rise.

She was drawn to the woman's remains.

The crows fell silent.

Renee's thoughts fell silent.

A solitary question rose to the forefront of her mind, asserted itself, and demanded attention:

"Should I have helped?

"No! The female should've taken personal responsibility for itself.

"Should I have helped?

"No! Only the fittest deserve to survive.

"Should I have helped?

"No! It should've helped itself.

"Should I have helped?

"Should I have helped?

"Should I have helped?"

THE DAY AFTER THE NIGHT BEFORE

> "Learning comes about when the
> competitive spirit has ceased."
> **JIDDU KRISHNAMURTI**

It was midday by the time Renee awoke.

The first thing she saw was a white rabbit, which vanished as soon as it appeared.

The second thing she saw was the man, who was chomping down on an apple.

Renee approached him from behind, startling him, and causing him to drop his meal.

Without understanding what she was doing, or why she was doing it, Renee squatted, collected the apple and offered it to the man.

He froze. He didn't breathe, his heart didn't beat, he didn't twitch or sway or shake. He remained in this state of stony paralysis for just under a second, snapped, and with one swift movement, which was too quick to see, he grabbed his apple and shoved our Renee to the ground.

Renee scolded herself:

"Why on earth did I do that?"

She felt as though another person had taken up residence inside her, seized control of her limbs and forced her to do something she would have never done herself. It petrified her. She feared what she might do next.

The man looked livid, and Renee didn't blame him:

"If I was in its position, I'd have wanted to take personal responsibility and retrieve my apple myself. I'd be furious if another me had gotten in my way. Mad!"

"Oh Renee, how could I be so... Aaagh!"

She felt she had no choice but to exert her individuality.

Since the man had pushed her away, Renee felt compelled to pull him towards her. The man closed his eyes, so Renee opened hers. She planted a kiss on his cheek; sucking him down, greedily, like a thirsty animal who had just discovered a well.

Renee smiled.

The man frowned.

Renee said "Sorry".

The man remained silent.

Renee preened herself; bending over and winking, seductively, like Marilyn Monroe.

The man ignored her.

Renee gestured to eat.

The man stopped eating.

Renee nibbled an apple.

The man devoured one.

Renee upped her pace. The man upped his pace. Renee grabbed a second apple. The man grabbed a third.

Pips, cores and stems fell like organic confetti.

Renee imagined her screen overhead, and watched it keep score: Three-two to the man. Five-four to Renee. Eleven-ten. Sixteen-fifteen.

She watched her Apple Eating Ranking climb into the top thousand... The top hundred... The top ten.

Her belly swelled and her stomach rumbled, but Renee didn't care. She stretched her arm above her head, winced, picked another apple, panted, and pulled it towards her mouth.

She collapsed, placed the apple between her teeth, and ate it without using her hands.

Renee had eaten eighteen apples, but the man had eaten twenty-one.

She discovered a hidden reserve of energy, leaped to her feet, grabbed three apples and ingested them with erotic fury. She fell to her knees, clutched her stomach, choked, spat out some pith, spat out some peel, looked up at the man and wheezed:

"I'm done, me damn it. Twenty-one all!"

The man clutched his ribs as he lumbered around the tree. He needed a single apple to win. But, bent out of shape, and unable to lift his neck, he couldn't locate the remaining apples, which were nestled in the uppermost branches.

He collapsed.

After several moments of stomach sounds, belly clutching, deep breathing, puffing, gasping and coughing; the man finally looked at our Renee. He hesitated, turned away, clawed his fingers through the earth, composed himself, turned back towards Renee, gazed into her eyes and smiled.

Renee smiled.

The man laughed.

Renee laughed.

The man turned away.

***

Renee ran her fingers through her hair. They made it two centimetres before getting entangled. Her nose felt crumbly to the touch. Her armpits smelled of vinegar and leftover meat.

She ambled over to a stream, washed herself, drank some water and returned to her tree.

A soft haze ambled across the meadow: Ethereal, mossy and brash. The grass bent in the breeze, but the shrubbery refused to budge. A lone star seemed embarrassed about its place in the daytime sky. A lone cricket chirruped for several minutes.

The afternoon lasted for several hours.

Without any jobs to complete, any desire to work, or any screens to distract her; Renee was left in a state of unmolested stillness. She watched a fox throw some food to a comrade, and observed a group of ants, safe in the knowledge there were still a few apples in the tree, and sure in her belief that the man would soon be her friend.

The hollowness of time gave way to the denseness of self-reflection.

Renee's eyes couldn't escape the lure of the woman's skull; upturned, shorn of its flesh, with a face which positively screamed.

She had visions of the night before: Of the wolves closing in, her heart pounding, the woman screaming, running, falling; the wolves bounding, leaping, biting; flesh yanked from flesh, limb torn from limb; bones cracking, blood spraying, life succumbing, fading, vanishing; leaving nothing in its wake, not even a perfunctory acknowledgement that a person had once existed.

This vision repeated itself ad infinitum. Whenever it stopped, a crow cawed, triggering Renee's memory, and forcing her to experience the ordeal again.

She questioned every detail: Did the woman's head droop to the left or the right? Did one wolf kill her or two? Were there really eight wolves? Was she sure there was a woman? Could she trust her senses at all?

The more she doubted the previous night's events, the more she filled with fear, horror, anger, guilt and shame. She was caught in a trap of negative emotions, unable to be grateful she'd survived, and unwilling to believe things would improve.

Her face turned purple, she kicked a clod of grass and embarked on an angry outburst:

"It's my fault the female died... I could be next! I deserve it for not trying to help. I will be next! I'm slow and feeble, with blunted teeth and flimsy nails. How am I to survive in this world of fangs, claws, horns and tusks? I'm going to die. I can't make it on my own!"

Renee wanted to curl up inside her pod, speak to her avatars, check Facebook, tweet, manage her debt, analyse her rankings, look for employment and complete a job: Anything to keep her mind from the previous night's events:

"I can't do it, any of it. My things are all in town."

She invented new distractions: Comparing the size of her fingers, counting the hairs on her thighs, and pacing between the trees; lifting her knees slightly higher with each passing step, until she found herself stomping on the spot.

She muttered:

"I don't get this. Any of it. I need to go home, where everything is safe."

She was struggling to breathe:

"Oh, what never-ending emptiness! Oh, what boundless ocean of doubt!"

She felt disconnected from life. She no longer dreamed of repaying her debt, buying a pod or retiring. She'd lost hope of finding 'Mum'.

"*I am what I own.*"

"I own nothing. I'm nothing!"

"*I shall be happy at all times.*"

"I'm not happy. I'm not."

"*I'm the only I, better than all I-Others.*"

"I-Others don't care! It just doesn't matter."

She worried about the man, the wolves and the apples; the cold, dark and rain. She worried about the meaninglessness of existence, London, her I-Friends, avatars, rankings, work and pod:

"I want to go home. I need to go home. I will have internet access! I will have cheese on toast!"

Her mind was set.

She stood up and turned to leave. But, as she rose, she caught sight of the man, who was also about to depart. He was also breathing sporadically, wearing a crabby expression that revealed his inner torment:

"I'm not alone. It's suffering as much as me!"

Renee noticed the man's pectorals. She saw the smooth contours of his abdominal muscles, which bulged beneath his shirt; stretching it taut and revealing his carnal form.

As if reading her mind, the man pulled his shirt up over his head, exposing his shiny torso. Renee removed her shirt. The man removed his trousers and underwear. Renee did the same.

They stood there, slack-jawed, staring at each other from afar:

"It looks nothing like I-Sex. Not so… Fake. Much more… Real. Much more… Appealing. I have to have it! I have to have it now!"

She clutched her vagina, pulled her clitoris and rubbed it from side to side. She panted; caressing the man with her eyes; following the contours of his armpit, waist and leg; exploring his feet, returning up his thigh, and fixing her gaze on his penis.

They stood there, several meters apart, masturbating together and squealing with tantric delight:

"Have to have it!"

"Have to cum!"

"Yes!"

"Yes! Yes! Yes!"

They gawked and jerked and screamed, trembled, stared into each other's eyes, reached for the heavens and came as one:

"Yes!"

"Yes! Yes! Yes!"

They sleepwalked together and collapsed on the floor.

Renee exhaled happiness:

"Is this what I've been searching for? It might just be!

"Hmm... Maybe I'll wait till tomorrow, before returning home. I mean, what harm can come from one more night?"

A second star appeared amidst the waxy twilight.

The man yawned.

Renee yawned, empathetically, without realising the two yawns were linked.

***

When the wolves approached that night, Renee and the man were asleep beneath the apple tree. The moon's craters were exposed by a low, claret glow. The wind whistled in broken stanzas.

The wolves smelled of an old butcher's shop; of blood on ice, raw meat and sprigs of parsley. Their breath was less clammy than before, but just as vaporous. It made the air feel like broth.

Renee awoke before the man. She grabbed hold of a branch and pulled herself up into the tree.

The wolves closed in.

This one was open-mouthed. Its teeth glistened and its tongue hung loose from its lips. This one was pensive. Narrow-eyed and pointy-nosed, it appeared to be assessing the scene. This one looked hungry. This one looked menacing and mean.

The man shot up, shaken awake by the presence of imminent danger.

"No," he shouted in his kittenish voice. But he lacked the presence of mind to kick stones at the wolves, as he'd done the night before. He just stood there, in a drowsy daze: Immobile, naked and inactive.

The wolves closed in.

Renee shook a branch. Its leaves fell like emerald snow.

She picked an apple, threw it at a wolf, and watched it miss its target. She threw a second apple, which hit the biggest wolf.

It whimpered, more out of shock than pain; making a high-pitched sound that faded to a hush.

Renee threw a third apple, missed, and threw a fourth, which hit the wolf.

It took two steps back.

"Ha!" the man grunted, with a coquettish tenderness that betrayed his intent.

Renee giggled, shook the branch, threw some more apples and jumped down; landing spread-eagle in front of the man:

"I'll eat it and it for breakfast!"

The wolves took a small step back.

Renee jolted forwards. Her hands were outstretched and her teeth were exposed.

The first wolf turned, the others turned, and they all skipped away; disappearing into the long grass, which bent outwards, forming rivulets and waves.

The attack had lasted less than two minutes.

Renee couldn't believe what she'd done. Once again, she felt as though another person had seized control of her body. It scared her more than the thought of death itself.

On edge, supersensitive to every sound and motion, she spun around to face the man. He was dressing, hurriedly, catching his foot on his boxer shorts, almost tripping, almost falling, shunting his trousers up his legs and grabbing his shirt.

He looked more dead than alive:

"Do that? Protect I-Differents? But why? What sort of competition is this? Makes no sense. Must have my pod. My dear avatars! Podsville here I come!"

He grabbed Renee's gas mask and ran.

A crow gave chase.

Renee gave chase; struggling through the shrubbery, as thorns scratched her shins and pollen invaded her nostrils.

She stopped, after less than twenty metres, and allowed the man to escape:

"Let it go, Renee. Just because it's a failure doesn't mean I should be. I can be stronger. I can be the best! I won't be like it. No way! I'll stay, just to exert my individuality. I'll be different. I'll – win – life!"

SURVIVAL OF THE FITTEST

"Communities which include the greatest number
of the most sympathetic members will flourish."
CHARLES DARWIN

Renee looks like she's escaped from an asylum.

Her eyes are sunken, surrounded by puffy, charcoal-coloured skin. It takes a preposterous effort to pry them open. When she does, she looks reproachful and cruel.

Her body looks cadaverous. It doesn't look gaunt, as such, but it does look rather lifeless.

Her nails are full of grit.

Her skin is grazed.

Observing her like this makes me want to leave, go to bed, and wipe the whole sorry scene from my mind. But, beloved friend, I simply can't do it. And I guess you shouldn't either. For our Renee is having a revelation. A new chapter is about to begin…

***

The meadow was laden with far too many nightmares for Renee to bear. Whenever she looked across its grassy expanse, she thought of the woman being torn to shreds, the man abandoning her, and her own descent into doubt.

Her stomach was feeling the effects of her apple-eating contest. Filled with malic acid, it was churning and making sounds.

A deer was grazing, a bird was eating a worm, and some ants were carrying a twig.

"Hang on a darn-totting mo… It and it aren't ill. The four-leggers don't overeat. The four-leggers know just how much to take! The wingers don't post pictures online. The wingers live in the moment. Each bug understands its place in the whole. The bugs work together!"

She jumped up and began to shout:

"I need a furry beast pack! I'm going to find it. Mum! I will find it. I – will – win – life!"

Renee looked around, sniffed the air and waited for inspiration.

The last remaining crow flew north towards the motorway.

"Ah yes, that's got to lead somewhere."

Renee dressed, left, scrambled up the embankment and climbed onto the tarmac expanse. It was eight lanes wide, cracked and overgrown, with white paint still visible in places. A rust-bitten sign, whose corners curled inwards, displayed lines marked "M25" and "A1".

Renee approached a windowless car, climbed inside, clutched the steering wheel, stepped on the brake and purred:

"Broom-broom. Broom-broom. Roar! Eeeek!!!"

It reminded her of a game she'd played in her pod, but never quite understood:

"I'm the best at this. Roar! Eeeek! Ten points to Renee!"

She left the car, continued down the motorway, took the slip road and entered a hanger marked "Welcome Break: South Mimms".

Renee had never seen anything like it. It wasn't made of glass, like the West End Industrial Estate. It wasn't otherworldly, like the homes she'd passed in London. It felt weird: Soulless, vacuous and light. Yet Renee felt a strange attraction to that place. She couldn't help but enter.

She gazed, open mouthed, as she wandered past a series of units filled with slanting shelves, fridges and price tags. You might call them "Shops". But Renee had never seen a shop. To her, that place was a trippy wonderland, like a scene in a science fiction film.

She ambled this way and that, stroking the metal railings and glass displays, throwing magazines into the air and dancing a tango with a naked mannequin.

Some of the brands amazed her.

"Subway," she whispered. "KFC. Waitrose."

She spotted something she recognized:

"Have a break. Have a Kit Kat."

This poster made her hum:

"Nike: Just do it.

"Yes! I can have Kit Kats. I can have Nike. I can just do it. Anything is possible if I believe in it enough!"

She skipped from one shop to another, danced down the aisles and jinked between the tills. She spent two hours in that place, before finally forcing herself to leave:

"Furry beast pack. 'Mum'. Must stick to the task at hand."

She crossed a bridge and walked down a country road.

The trees here seemed to be sinking into early retirement, hanging low, haughtily, yet possessing what you might call "Fairy-tale qualities". This one had leaves which hunkered down its trunk, this one looked like a dancing lady, and this one reflected the sky.

Renee was thunderstruck. These "Brown poles with green hats" filled her with woozy-eyed wonder. She stroked them, ran her nose up their bark and inhaled their sappy scent.

She walked past a turning. She didn't give it a second thought, continued, stopped, and realised something was awry. She tiptoed back, turned down the lane and scratched her head:

"These walls aren't cracked. These houses aren't overgrown. They look almost... Almost... Alive."

Six semi-detached houses stood either side of the lane. Some were whitewashed, some were covered in ivy. They were charismatic, slightly ramshackle, but homely and loved. This one had tiles which zigzagged across the roof, cutting triangles out of the sky. This one had windowpanes which framed the gravelly road. This one was a tapestry of original features and unplanned appendages; iron railings as old as the house, and walls that had been painted at various times.

Renee saw the invisible people inside: Cooking, talking, joking and laughing. She listened to their high-pitched laughter and smelled the food on their stoves.

A door swung open and a middle-aged woman stepped through. She was only wearing one item of clothing: An animal's fur, which stretched from her shoulders to her knees. She was bulbous, with blackened teeth and a blotched complexion. She didn't appear to have had any plastic surgery at all.

Renee couldn't help but judge her harshly.

"Howdy, stranger!" the woman sang. "Welcome to our humble abode. Why don't you come inside and join us for a cup of camomile tea?"

Renee was startled. She had to compose herself, and fix her feet in position, before she could even think about forming a response.

A second woman, who was naked from the bellybutton up, appeared behind the first woman's shoulder. Renee liked the feathers in her ears, and appreciated the effort she'd put into braiding hair, but was appalled by that woman's immodesty.

Her face wrinkled into a grimace and she covered her nose with her hand.

The second woman cheered:

"Well hello, sister! You're more than welcome here."

Renee took a small step back.

Behind her, a second door opened and an elderly man stepped out. He was liver-spotted and grey-haired, with a walking stick and a stoop:

"Hello there, sweetie. You must be shattered. Now don't you be shy, we'd love to welcome you in."

A third door opened and another man appeared. He was wearing a three-piece suit, held together by a random collection of patches and pins:

"Oh, what a pleasant surprise! Do be an angel and come inside for a lovely slice of cake."

The other doors opened with a short staccato rhythm. Twelve people stepped through. They all looked different. They all peppered the air with warm salutations.

Renee didn't know how to react.

She'd been comfortable when taking the lead herself, pushing human contact on her companions in the meadow. But now that other people were controlling the narrative, she felt helpless, and was unable to utter a word. She'd been close to saying "Hello" to the first woman, believed sincerely she would've done it, and would've entered her home; but she was overwhelmed by the sheer presence of so many people, and by the outpouring of so much love. Yes, she wanted company, and yes, she wanted love; but not this much company, and not this much love. She was overwhelmed these people's use of strange words such as "We", "You" and "Us"; by their bizarre appearances and peculiar clothes.

A part of her thought, "This is my furry beast pack". She wanted it to be true.

But a larger part of her thought, "It's not real. It can't be. Individuals don't live together like this."

She thought she might have imagined the entire scene. She couldn't believe the people here genuinely wanted to meet her, assumed they were faking their love, had some sort of ulterior motive, and might even be a threat.

"It's not real!" she screamed. "It and it aren't real! None of it is!"

She backtracked, span around, turned the corner, stopped herself and hunched over. She panted. Her breath turned white. Moisture blurred her vision.

***

After a few minutes had passed, Renee recognized the scent of her own perfume, even though she hadn't applied it in days.

Confused, she turned and saw a young girl who reminded her of I-Original. She was also short, with pigtails and freckles. She hadn't yet reached the age at which our bodies start to reflect our personalities. Her skin was still smooth and her face was still symmetric. She didn't possess a single blemish or scar. Her eyes were inquisitive but not wise, and her forehead was free from judgmental lines.

Renee drew great comfort from the smell of the cinnamon bun this girl was holding. But she could only lift her shoulders, open her palms and shrug. She was unable to form any sort of facial expression.

The girl held up the bun:

"Take it. It's yours."

Renee touched it and acknowledged it was real.

The girl placed her hand on Renee's arm.

Being touched so tenderly, for the first time in her life, gave Renee a momentous thrill. It spread warmth throughout her body, softened her skin, massaged her organs and reddened her face. Oxytocin flooded her amygdala, washing her fears and anxieties away. Painkilling endorphins soothed her aching feet.

Renee found the strength she needed to reply:

"What... Err... What does 'Yours' mean?"

"It belongs to you."

"'You'?"

"Yes. It's not for me, or any other doo-doo-head, it's yours. Om nom nom nom nom."

"It's mine?"

"Yes. Take it. Take every last incy-wincy bit of it."

"No... I can't."

"Cowardy custard! Fraidy cat! Scaredy pants! Why can't you take it? Huh? Why?"

"Because... Because I don't deserve it. I haven't done anything to earn it."

"'Earn'? That's not a real word!"

"Is too! I need to work, so I can afford to buy this bun."

"'Work'? What's 'Work'?"

"Anything: Moving stuff, breaking stuff, writing reports, running, skipping, doing star-jumps. It... *You...* You name it, I can do it. I'm the best!"

The girl giggled. It was a flirtatious giggle, one part ditsy and one part coy. Her cheeks inflated and her freckles stretched, becoming wider but fainter with each additional snigger:

"You can do some star-jumpies if you like."

"Yes! I'm the best at star-jumps. How many shall I do?"

The girl ummed and ahhed before answering:

"Twelfty!"

Renee performed one hundred and twenty star-jumps.

The girl held out the bun, giggled, and pulled it away:

"Nah, that was easy-peasy, lemon squeezy. Now: Take ten ickle steps in that direction, touch your tum-tum, do a roly-poly, sniff the sky, do a curtsey and sit on your botty."

Renee did as she was told.

The girl held out the bun, giggled, and was about to pull it away. But she was stopped short by her mother, who had just turned around the corner.

The girl's mother was a deep-set woman with a sunken brow, a turban of auburn hair and a pair of bulbous eyes. Apron strings cut unnecessarily deep into the cellulite which wrapped itself around her midriff. The scent of candle wax and flour clung to her fawnlike ankles, which were struggling to support her more-than-ample frame:

"Curie, honey, I think our friend can have her cake now, don't you?"

Renee wanted to ask about these strange new words: "Her" and "Our". But she was hungry, and the bun smelled delicious, so she took it and began to eat.

The mother smiled:

"How do you feel, my love?"

"My stomach is satisfied, my taste buds are buzzing, but I do feel a little gassy, and expect I'll fart very soon. My limbs are slightly hollow from my walk. Yes, there it is, I've farted... Hmm... All this talking is making me sleepy. And... And... Am I supposed to ask how it is? I mean, how *you* are? Is that how this works? It'll... *You'll* have to excuse me, I've never done this before."

The mother smiled:

"Yes, asking how I am is lovely. Thank-you. I'm very happy indeed."

"Why?"

"Because I've made a new friend."

"Really? Who?"

"You, silly. Now do come inside. We've made you a lovely bath."

Renee turned red:

"No, no, no! This isn't real! It can't be. It doesn't make any sense. Why are it… Why are *you* being so nice? So welcoming? You should be more selfish, more natural. Stop teasing me, you horrible, selfless individual!"

The mother's face became transparent. Capillaries drew blue patterns on her cheeks, and her teeth could be seen through her skin.

Renee covered her face:

"Sorry. It's just… It's… None of this makes any sense."

The mother nodded:

"It doesn't, does it? If I were in your position, I'd feel exactly the same. But let's not worry about what does and doesn't make sense. We can deal with that sort of stuff another time."

***

After Renee had bathed, she was shown up to a bedroom in a converted loft.

It was a place she found hard to judge.

The fact there was no lift, made Renee snort with derision. These people didn't have internet access, avatars or screens. Renee didn't know whether to pity them or mock them.

The bedroom itself was double the height of Renee's pod, with ten times the floor space. Renee could stand up without knocking her head. She could pace between the bed, pool table, bookshelf and cupboard. She thought she was being spoilt:

"But… No… Something's not right here. How could it and it… How could *they* afford such a place? It and it… *They* don't even know words such as 'Work' or 'Earn'. How could they earn such a place without working? I've worked my entire life and haven't even bought a pod. It's not fair. It's not right. I shouldn't trust these individuals one bit."

She looked through the window:

"How could any I-Other… *Anyone* deserve such a view? It's divine. It's just not right!"

She was confused, angry, shocked, bemused, unsure and unsteady. She would've thrown a fit, had she not been distracted by a man who was crawling down the street.

I'm afraid to say I simply can't find the words to express the sheer vulgarity of this man. I positively hate him! He turns my stomach and leaves me rigid with disgust. It baffles me to think that anyone could like him.

This man, this naked animal, was behaving like a dog; prancing around on all fours, as if guarding the houses; eating raw meat, headfirst from a bowl; panting, growling, barking, howling, lunging and pawing the earth. He even looked like a dog. His body was covered in hair. His limbs were shortened and bent from a lifetime spent crawling on all fours. He couldn't have walked upright if he'd tried. It had been said that his senses were impeccable, but I'm not inclined to believe such hearsay myself.

Renee ran her hand down the window, as if stroking this mutt man's fur. Her eyes took on a veiled look. She felt she'd discovered something vitally important, but couldn't be sure what it was.

She stood there, transfixed, watching the mutt man come and go, bark, sit in a triangular fashion, cock his leg and urinate on a plant. She would've stayed there all night had Curie's mother, Simone, not knocked on the door and entered:

"We're going to the longhouse. You don't have to join us, but you're more than welcome to come…"

***

The 'Longhouse' was a converted thirteenth-century church, with walls made of flint rubble and red brick. The pews had been pushed to the front, and a fire pit had been dug between two lines of white pillars.

Over a hundred villagers were spread across the floor, dressed in a whiffy assortment of deerskins, sheepskins, woollen jumpers and patched up clothes. The mutt man, that horrific waste of flesh and bone, was curled up with two real dogs; keeping an eye on our Renee, who was sitting between Curie and Simone.

Renee perused the other villagers: This man named Kipling, with a bushy moustache, who recited a poem called "If". This woman named Pankhurst, with boyish hair, who told a fable about a turtle. And this girl named Boudicca, with ginger locks, who passed out cookies and pies.

It seemed to Renee that everyone was a true individual. They all wore different clothes, in different ways, and they all had different roles.

A sudden burst of noise fizzed in Renee's ears. Every man had begun to sing. Every woman replied. Drums tapped, lutes strummed and cymbals smashed. Renee's arm-hair stood erect. She pressed her palms against the floor and lifted herself into the air.

The music stopped.

Everyone clapped.

A longhaired youth played a folk song on his guitar. A barbershop quartet harmonised a short ditty. A choir sang "Freedom".

A silver-haired old man rose to his feet. The deep rivulets on his forehead softened and then hardened; rising and falling like waves. His beard seemed to pulsate.

Everyone cheered:

"Hello, Socrates!"

Renee stuttered the word "Hello" a second after everyone else.

As the group talked about the communal grain supply, and the leaky roof in house number seven, Renee became increasingly aware of the eyes which were glaring at her from every direction. Some people were glancing at her briefly, then turning away. A middle-aged man was staring down his crooked nose. A small boy pinched Renee's thigh. A young girl pulled her hair.

Renee yelped.

This noise startled the mutt man, who rocketed out of his basket, bounded across the room and leaped towards our Renee. He would've planted his teeth into her neck, had he not been bundled away by a group of heroic women.

There! I told you he was beyond contempt, and now you've seen it for yourself. His vulgarity can't be denied!

Renee's heart was a blurry drumroll; a melee of rumbling beats. She'd skidded back into Pankhurst, knocking her tea to the floor, and was fanning her face to cool down.

Socrates turned to Renee:

"My dear, please excuse poor Darwin. He's a good boy. Well, he is most of the time. It's just... Well, he was abandoned as a baby, back in London, and would've died had he not been raised by wild dogs. You may have noticed how he acts like a dog. Well, he has these uncontrollable instincts to protect us, his pack, from what he sees as outsiders and threats.

"Oh no, dear girl, please don't think of yourself as an outsider or a threat! You're one of us. By Jove, you surely are! You're welcome to stay for as long you like."

A gentle rumble of approval meandered across the room. Some people said "Hear! Hear!" Others nodded. A small boy clapped. A small girl blew a raspberry.

"Well, we didn't want to put you on the spot like this. But, seeing as you've grabbed our attention, is there anything you'd like to ask? You don't have to, of course, it's up to you."

Renee raised her eyes.

Soothed by the grandfatherly warmth of this man, she forgot her inhibitions and asked the first question which popped into her head:

"Why is its... Why is *your* grass green?"

Socrates frowned:

"Our grass? Green? Well, my dear, all grass is green."

Renee shook her head:

"No! It can't be. Grass is blue!"

Socrates smiled. It was a sprightly smile; cherry red in places, leathery at the seams, with a distinct air of age-ripened vivacity:

"Yes, my dear, grass is blue. We have special, green grass, because that's the way we like it."

"Oh. It and it... *You're* individuals?"

"Well, yes, dear girl, I suppose we are!"

Socrates gave Renee the time she needed to think of another question.

"Why did the furry beasts eat the female I met in the meadow? Why couldn't it and it... Why couldn't *they* eat meat?"

"Well, people *are* made of meat."

"What? No! Meat is made in giant vats. I've viewed it with my own Plenses!"

Socrates beamed:

"It is? How fascinating! You'll have to tell us all about that."

Renee nodded. Her questions were coming thick and fast:

"Which one of it and it... Which one of *you* is 'Mum'?"

Most of the women raised their hand.

Renee frowned:

"It and it... *You're*... You're all 'Mum'? But... The thing is... I'm on a mission to find 'Mum'. Hmm. Perhaps I've succeeded. I mean, I was only searching for one 'Mum' and I've found over thirty, so... Yes! I've got the high score!"

Frowns turned into smiles, which turned into laughter. Simone patted Renee's back and Curie squeezed her thigh.

Socrates explained:

"A mum, or 'Mother', is someone who's given birth to a baby."

"Given birth?"

"Produced a baby. Created a child, a person. Here, after a woman has created a baby, they care for them, house them and feed them. Simone is a mum. Just look at how she cares for Curie."

Renee felt her head vibrate. It buzzed with a thousand questions about Babytron robots, baby creation, Simone and Curie:

"So, which one of it and it... Which one of *you* is my mother? Which one of you created me?"

Heads dropped and shoulders shrugged.

"Why? Why would any I-Other... Why would *anyone* help a child? Why would anyone help anyone else? Why are it and it... Why are *you* doing this? Why are you helping me? Why? It doesn't make any sense. Whatever happened to personal responsibility? Don't you wish you were self-made?"

Murmurs filled the hall.

Socrates smiled:

"Would you like to hear our story? Perhaps it'll help you to understand the way we act..."

Renee nodded.

"Well then, dear girl, I think we should hand over to our village historians: Chomsky and Klein."

Chomsky was everything Klein was not. He was large, whilst she was small. He had wild eyebrows and a bristly beard. She was completely hairless. Chomsky was naturally overbearing, although prone to the occasional outburst of boyish immaturity. Klein was diminutive and stern. But they were both united by their common love of history, and their common love of pickled eggs.

Klein began:

"Our foremothers and forefathers..." She gestured in the direction of an elderly couple. "Moved to South Mimms shortly after the Great Consolidation. There were only thirteen of us back then. We were the last trade unionists in the land."

Renee frowned:

"Trade unionists?"

"Yes," Chomsky explained. "Trade unions were organisations through which workers united to demand better pay and conditions. They achieved great things, you know; securing paid holidays, maternity leave and the two-day weekend. But they were linked to Socialism..."

Renee's jaw dropped open.

Klein smiled:

"Socialists believed in society. Ah... Yes... Society is where two or more people come together to be social... Umm... To interact, like we're interacting now. This group is a society. Living with other people, in a society, makes us 'Socialists'."

Renee almost punched the air:

"Yes! Yes, yes, yes! That's exactly what I thought I wanted. I wanted to interact with I-Others... with *people*. To be a *Social Thingy*. Yes, a *Socialist*. Although I must say it feels awfully strange now it's actually happening."

Chomsky nodded:

"It feels strange because it goes against everything you've ever experienced. You were born into an individualistic system. And, under individualism, there's no such thing as society. People don't interact."

Klein continued:

"When the Individualists came to power, in 1979, they made it their goal to destroy society. They waged war on the trade unionists, calling us 'The enemy within'... They won... By the time of the Great Consolidation, there were only thirteen of us left."

"The Great Thirteen!" echoed Chomsky.

"The Great Thirteen," mumbled the room.

Klein shrugged:

"We'd lost the battle of ideas. And, whilst wanted to stay and help, the people in London wouldn't let us. Even though they were suffering, they wanted to work hard and take personal responsibility for themselves."

Chomsky continued:

"We were under enormous pressure to conform, you know. We had no property, no work, and feared jail or worse. But then we met our saviour, Anita Podsicle, the owner of Podsicle Industries; an eccentric woman, who owned a quarter of Britain.

"Anita had a keen interest in social anthropology. As an experiment, she gave us this village and observed us from afar. We were her hobby, I suppose: Her little pet tribe of Socialists.

"In the early days, Anita used to invite us to her palace. We always answered her calls, because we feared she'd send us to London if we refused. But those meetings became more infrequent by the year. And, when Anita passed away, we lost touch with her heir and son."

Renee nodded:

"Yes... But... That's just fine and dandy, it explains a lot, but it doesn't really answer my question."

Chomsky and Klein frowned in unison. The lines on Chomsky's forehead appeared to extend across onto Klein's.

"None of that explains why it and it... Why *you're* treating me like this. Why are you helping me? Why are you being so kind???"

Renee's face hardened.

Klein's face softened:

"When we first arrived here, we established a library, and read up on how humans had lived before there were any nations. It turned out they survived by operating in teams. Cooperating. So that's what we did: We built our village on the principle of cooperation."

Chomsky took the baton:

"We want to help you because we like to help, you know. It's what we do: We cooperate. We operate as a team. We share.

"We've been waiting decades to welcome someone from London. You're the first person to make it this far, and we're incredibly excited to meet you. We want to share with you. It's in our nature to share. Sharing is the natural order of things!"

Beloved friend: Sometimes it's easier to fool a person than it is to convince them they've been fooled. Whilst Renee had done her best to understand the group's history, this last statement was a step too far.

"It and it are wrong!" she shouted, whilst getting to her feet.

"It and it are all wrong!" she bellowed, whilst flinging out her hands; demanding to possess the space around her. "Sharing? 'The natural order of things'? What baloney!

"I view what it and it are like; crowding in here, snooping, prying, listening; squashing me, judging me, teasing me; trying to drive me insane with it and its crazy speech.

"It's lies! Lies, I tell it, lies! London isn't bad. I don't need saving. I *can* take personal responsibility. I have avatars which know what I want. I don't need books. I have the internet! I have access to all the information in the world! I have hundreds of computer games, thousands of virtual accessories, millions of I-Friends and more. I have calorie-substitute, protein pâté and enamel cordial. I have my own scent, my own clothes, my own everything. I'm a true individual. I'm happy! I have all the happiness gas I need. It name it, I have it. I have so much more than any I-Other here. It and it should want what *I* have, should want *my* help. I'm Renee Ann Blanca. I'm the best!"

Renee ran out of words to speak.

She'd lost track of what she was saying, and had only continued because she thought she'd look ridiculous if she were to stop.

Her legs wobbled, she swayed, and crumpled to the ground.

Curie massaged her shoulders.

Socrates scratched his beard:

"My dear girl, what you say is truly captivating. I'm sure I'm not alone when I say I'd be fascinated to hear more about your I-Friends and protein pâté. I'm sure there's a lot you could teach us. In your own time, of course. When you're ready."

Heads began to nod.

"Well, what I feel my friends meant to say, if I can be so bold as to interpret, is that we're all excited to meet you. You said you hadn't just succeeded, you'd got the high score. And, do you know what? I think you're right. Dear girl: You broke the darn tootin' scale!"

Renee looked up.

The pride she felt, which she couldn't understand, let alone describe, was like nothing she'd experienced before.

"Dear girl: We've been waiting decades for a Londoner to make it to our humble village. We prayed for your arrival, dreamed of your arrival, and almost gave up hope. But here you are! As sure as night follows day, here you are, in the flesh, stood in front of us all!

"Excuse us for our errors. We simply weren't expecting you to arrive *right here, right now*. We'd stopped believing. We thought everyone in London had died.

"That you survived in that Individutopia for so long, without human contact, without killing yourself, without starving... Well... Wow! Just wow! And that you escaped? No one has ever made it this far before. Renee: You're a hero. A real life, warm-blooded, rip-roaring hero! One of a kind! The ultimate individual!

"You asked why we helped you. Well, we helped you because you deserved to be helped! You're special. The only person to escape from Individutopia. The only person to make it this far. The woman who broke the scale!

"Of course you deserve to be helped. You deserve every last

thing that comes your way!"

The villagers had risen to their feet. They were clapping their hands, stamping, dancing, smiling and cheering:

"Renee! Renee! Renee!"

Whipped up by the sheer ebullience of it all, Renee joined in. She danced amidst the melee and cheered along with the crowd.

Even after she'd been carried home, carried up to bed and left alone for the night; her head still rang with the sound of those cheers. Her mind was still filled with visions of that day's events. For the first time since leaving London, Renee didn't worry about food, the future, wolf-dogs or the weather. She didn't miss her pod, avatars or work. She didn't pretend that I-Green was by her side. She smiled, fell into a blissful slumber, and dreamed a hundred dreams.

THE ONLY CONSTANT IS CHANGE

> "People don't change. They
> reveal who they really are."
> **ANONYMOUS**

The seven people who lived with Simone were gathered around the breakfast table; helping themselves to bread, which Simone had baked; eggs, which Curie had gathered; and some honey from the village's hive.

Renee asked a question she'd been pondering since her arrival:

"If you don't work, how do you buy the things you need to survive?"

Simone smiled. It was a dense smile, which started deep within her eyes, trickled down her nose and illuminated her entire face:

"We don't 'Buy' things, we make them.

"We're lucky in many ways. We have plenty of houses, so we don't need to build. We repair and reuse our clothes. The big thing for us is food. But we have lots of land, and Mother Nature treats us well. Some people enjoy caring for animals. Others take great pride in planting and harvesting crops. For them, it's a hobby, not a chore. No one 'Works', per se. For us, the hard-work mentality is a slave's mentality. We *want* to contribute, to take *Collective Responsibility*, but it's up to us to choose what we do. We only spend about twenty hours a week doing the sort of things you might class as 'Work', but we don't consider it a burden."

"But… Hang on… What happens if someone does consider it a burden? What if they don't want to contribute?"

"They don't have to."

"And then what?"

"If they don't like our ways, they're free to leave."

"Has anyone done that?"

"Once. A guy named Tyler marched on London back in the

early years."

"What happened?"

"He returned after four days, drained of life, and died a few weeks later."

"Oh."

Renee tapped the table:

"So how do *you* contribute?"

"We forage for wild food. In fact, we're going on a nature walk this morning. You're more than welcome to join us."

Renee nodded, stopped herself, and then frowned:

"Hang on... So, instead of working, you're going for a walk?"

Simone laughed:

"Yeah! We'll take our bags and spears, trek to some hidden spots, gather some food, maybe hunt an animal, and have a good old natter on the way."

"Oh."

"I think we'll start by heading to our favourite apple tree. Do you like apples?"

"Yes. Oh yes. But..."

Renee was hit by a sudden pang of guilt. Her heat rushed towards her core, and the rest of her body felt like it was melting away. It took an enormous effort, and no small part of courage, for her to admit what she'd done:

"This apple pole... *Tree*... Is it in a meadow near the giant road?"

Everyone nodded.

"Well... The thing is... I think I may have... You know, they're just apples, right? Well, they might not be. I mean... Maybe... Maybe that tree doesn't have any apples right now..."

Simone smiled:

"You mean to say... Oh, I see. Well that's fine. We know lots of other apple trees. Don't you worry about a thing!"

***

Renee was thrilled to see so many women as she ambled through South Mimms. Here was a hawk-faced lady, who was walking five dogs. Her clothes were covered in cat-hair and her pockets were full of ferrets. Here was a lady with a spherical neck, who was carrying a pitcher of milk. Over there stood a gaggle of chattering friends. To their right, some girls were playing hopscotch in the street.

Renee digested these scenes.

She noted that their lane was separated from the rest of the village by a small park and a patchwork of blurry allotments. A short road brought them to a pub, "The White Hart"; a faux-Tudor building, covered in white paint and black wood. Behind that pub, a hodgepodge of empty homes had sloping roofs and skew-whiff front gardens.

Renee meandered one way and then the other, bug-eyed, gawking at everything she passed. She stroked the brickwork and bark, listened to the sound of the wind, and inhaled the aromas of cut grass and burning wood.

***

When Simone passed her a satchel from the village store, a room attached to the longhouse, Renee stepped back and raised her palms:

"I can't... I... I... I've not done anything to earn them."

Simone rolled her eyes and laughed:

"Not this again. What are you like, Renee Ann?"

"Oh. I know. Sorry. It's just... This is all so new to me. I mean, I understand the logic, but the application... It's just... It feels like I'm breathing water and drinking the air."

Simone grinned:

"See if you can take this without a fuss. You can do it, my love, you can!"

Renee smiled, took the spear from Simone, took Curie's hand and followed her outside.

***

They stepped into a crowd.

"It seems you're popular," Simone explained. "Everyone wants to meet the messiah!"

Renee hid her head inside her shirt.

"Now, now. You're feeling a little intimidated, aren't you? Don't worry, my love, it's fine. You don't have to speak until you're ready."

Their group strolled past a jumble of shivery houses, green spaces, cows and windmills. A lonesome column of smoke rose, drunkenly, and was lost to the windless air.

By the time they left the village, that nasty little mutt man was bounding by Renee's side; indifferent to the frozen mud; wagging its bottom in the air and panting its vile, soppy breath.

Renee spoke out in a grandiloquent voice:

"I'm ready to answer a question!"

No one said a word.

Most of the villagers had questions to ask, but they didn't want to be so presumptuous as to speak first.

In such situations, it's usually the young, lacking the tremulous caution of old age, who are prepared to step into the light. This case was no exception.

An eleven-year-old broke the silence:

"How did you do it? Escape, I mean. How did you escape?"

Renee laughed:

"I walked."

"No one stopped you?"

"No. I suppose I'd always been free to leave, I'd just chosen not to."

"So why did you do it? I mean, why did you leave?"

"I wanted to meet another person."

"Oh. And you couldn't meet another person in London?"

"I'd never viewed another person in London."

"There aren't any people there?"

"Londoners wear Plenses, which stop them from viewing anyone else."

"What happened? To yours, I mean. What happened to yours?"

"I took them out."

The entourage gasped.

Kuti raised his hands:

"Amazing! We'd heard of people whose Plenses had fallen out, or who'd forgotten to put them in, but we thought they'd all gone mad. We'd never heard of anyone removing their Plenses by choice. That's... Prodigious! Incredible! Unique!"

The group stopped at a blackberry bush.

Renee answered their questions in turn; describing her Plenses, and explaining what happened when she removed them; describing her screen, debt, work, avatars, I-Friends, pod and rankings; the food she ate, the accessories she wore, and London town itself. She spoke about her Eureka Moment, escape, and journey to South Mimms.

By the time she was done, the villagers had filled several tubs with blackberries, filled three sacks with apples, gathered some stinging nettles, elderflowers, watercress, mushrooms and sorrel. They'd visited their traps and removed seven rabbits.

As they headed home, Renee was struck by another pang of guilt. Her stomach felt heavy and her limbs felt light.

"These people have given me so much," she thought. "They've fed, housed and bathed me; listened to me, taken me out, and taught me what food to eat. And what have I given them in return? Nothing! Absolutely nothing! It's not right. It's not fair."

She looked to nature for inspiration.

She saw a vole drink from a stream, and felt compelled to get water for her friends, but she didn't have any beakers or bottles. She listened to some birdsong, and thought about singing, but she worried she'd sing out of tune.

As they rounded a bend, she saw a cow lick her daughter clean. To Renee, it seemed like the most beautiful thing in the world: Natural, caring and wholesome. She turned to Simone, gripped her head and ran her tongue up the side of her face.

Simone pulled away, instinctively, donning a look which blended chagrin with confusion. But the mutt man reacted just as instinctively, and just as quickly; rising up on his hind legs, placing his paws on Renee's shoulder and licking her cheek with gay abandon.

Lost in the moment, oblivious to their friends, they licked each other clean. They continued licking, up and down, until they noticed that everyone was staring.

Renee immediately pulled away.

Silence fell from the sky.

The mutt man chased his bottom and curled up into a ball.

Simone smiled.

Her comrades guffawed.

***

Renee tried to explain:

"I wanted to contribute. I wanted to be a part of the group."

Simone responded with sensitive eyes:

"You don't feel like you're fitting in, do you? But you are! Believe me: *You are.*"

"I am?"

"Yes! Look at how you've stopped calling us 'It and it'."

"Oh."

"You're doing great."

Simone put her arm around Renee's shoulder and led her into the storeroom:

"Okay, my love, please pass me the spear."

Renee couldn't do it.

She'd never borrowed anything, never shared, and never returned something she'd liked. She found the concept completely alien. She winced. She knew she should return that weapon, but her hands refused to budge.

She held out the spear, Simone took it, but Renee pulled back.

Simone looked into Renee's eyes, which were blurry pink, paused, and let go.

"It's okay," she said. "It's okay. If I was in your position, I'd want to keep it too."

Simone's dulcet tones helped to massage Renee's mind. Her muscles relaxed, tensed, and then relaxed. Her grip loosened and she dropped the spear.

Simone beamed:

"Well done! Now come inside, my love, come inside."

Renee followed Simone into the longhouse, where they placed their bounty atop a set of wooden tables.

As soon as they were done, a bent-backed old lady, who smelled of chives, took their apples and put them in her trolley.

Incensed, feeling she'd been robbed, Renee grabbed three hessian sacks and stuffed them full with flour, cured pork, broccoli, lettuce and tomatoes. She took a fistful of cottage cheese and shoved it into her mouth.

No one said a word. They didn't need to. They had already formed a circle around our Renee. They were pointing their index fingers and blinking with aggressive speed.

Some curds dripped from Renee's lips.

Determined to push on through, she grabbed some carrots, shoved them into her pockets, and moved along the table.

The villagers closed in.

Renee's heart sank. She felt her strength implode, sucked in towards her core. Her limbs felt vaporous. Her hair felt hot.

Unsure what was happening, but sure she wanted it to stop, Renee removed her tomatoes and placed them on the table.

The villagers stepped back.

Renee returned the other vegetables.

The villagers lowered their arms.

Renee returned the pork and flour.

The villagers dispersed.

Curie gave Renee a high-five.

Simone smiled:

"That was amazing. *You* were amazing!"

"Ah... Ah... I was?"

"Yes!"

"I don't understand. I... I... What just happened?"

"Shame! The authority of public opinion! It's how we keep order. If someone takes too much, or gives too little, we shame them, to encourage them to change their ways."

"Oh."

"And that's what you did!"

"I did?"

"Yes, my love, yes. You realised you'd taken too much and corrected your mistake."

"Oh."

"You're one of us now."

"I am?"

"Yes! We appreciate having you around."

"But... But... I really don't understand what I did. That old lady took all my... All *our* apples. I was only copying her. How come she wasn't shamed?"

Simone laughed:

"Oh, old Wollstonecraft is a master baker, the best in the village. She'll turn those apples into yummy pies, which she'll bring back here tomorrow. Trust me: You haven't tried anything quite like a Wollstonecraft pie."

Renee thought for a moment, clicked her fingers, took a bag, and filled it with flour and cheese.

Simone scratched her head:

"What are you doing?"

"You mean, 'What are *we* doing?' *We're* going to make cheese on toast for the entire village. If that old lady can do it, so can we. Simone: We're going to be the best!"

***

After they'd eaten lunch, and baked some bread for the cheese on toast, Renee wandered off on her own. Being in the presence of so many people, for so long, had left her feeling jaded. She needed some time alone.

She observed village life from afar, like a tourist in a living museum.

Over here, a young woman was massaging some leather with artistic devotion. Over there, two men were milling grain; laughing, joking and throwing flour.

Renee recognised a couple from that morning's walk. They were sat beneath an oak, knitting jumpers, talking and smiling. It seemed to Renee that they were far more productive than she'd ever been, even though they didn't appear to be trying.

But it was the sight of four young mothers which inspired Renee the most.

She'd been thinking of that word, "Mum", ever since Socrates had explained what it meant. For Renee, it held a quixotic allure.

"Mum," she whispered, softly, rolling the word around her tongue. "Mother... Muh verr... Mum. Mother. Mum."

The mothers were sitting on a blanket. One was grooming her daughter; removing lice from her hair, before tying it in plaits. Another was breastfeeding her baby.

Renee had never seen anything like it. She flinched, covered her face, and spied on that woman from between the cracks in her fingers.

The women laughed.

Renee laughed.

She turned to face the children.

A young boy called to a young girl, inviting her to join their game. They agreed on a set of rules and began to play; creating chains of buttercups and daisies, chasing each other, catching each other, and placing those chains around each other's necks.

A toddler pointed at some flowers, which lay just beyond her reach. An older boy picked them and passed them to the toddler.

Seeing this, one of the mothers stood up, approached, and rewarded the boy with a cookie. He broke it apart and shared it amongst his friends.

This reminded Renee of Chomsky's strange statement:

"Sharing is the natural order of things."

Only here, it didn't seem so strange. It seemed natural. So natural, in fact, that it made Renee question her entire worldview.

Wishing to quash such doubts as quickly as she could, she approached a group of adults who were playing football. Inspired by the children, she asked if she could play.

Although she struggled to keep up, tripping over her feet and shinning the ball, she did break through on goal. It surprised her when she decided to pass rather than shoot. It surprised her even more when her teammates congratulated *her* and not the scorer.

She spent the rest of the evening talking with the other players, visiting the library and dancing in the longhouse.

When she returned home, she asked if she could sleep with Curie and Simone:

"I've spent my whole life sleeping alone. Tonight, I'd like to share a bed."

Curie nodded. Then she yawned.

Renee yawned back, empathetically, looked into Simone's eyes, stepped forwards and embraced her friend.

Every nerve ending in her body fizzed with tingly delight.

It was Renee's first ever hug, and it gave her an organic high. Oxytocin and dopamine gushed through her veins. Her cortisol levels reduced, washing her stress and tension away. Serotonin destroyed her loneliness. Endorphins blocked the pain receptors in her aching feet. Her blood pressure reduced, easing the pressure on her heart.

Renee felt wanted, needed, appreciated and loved.

THE LAST CUT IS THE DEEPEST

"Every new beginning comes from
some other beginning's end."
SENECA

Renee adjusted to communal life.

She hugged her housemates, shook hands with the villagers and patted other people's backs. Her love for Simone grew, and spread, until she felt a connection with almost everyone she met.

But the effects weren't purely psychological. Renee became healthier and more energetic. After a fortnight in South Mimms, she menstruated for the first time.

Her speech evolved. She learned the names of animals and trees, and began to use words such as "We", "Us", "You" and "Their".

She continued to go on nature walks; to scavenge, hunt and fish. She enjoyed it, most of the time, although she did fall into a state of shock when her group discovered the half-eaten remains of the man she'd met in the meadow. Her lips turned blue and she almost collapsed. But her friends came to her rescue; laying her down, lifting her legs and whispering supportive words.

Seeing that alpha male, unable to survive on his own, helped Renee to focus her mind. She made a concerted effort to help with every task; trying her hand at milking the cows, feeding the chickens, planting seeds, transferring plants, harvesting tomatoes and repairing some pipes.

But it was Renee's attitude to play which showed she'd truly evolved. She let go of her addiction to work, and found a way to live in the moment; talking, joking and laughing with the other villagers; applying makeup to the other girls; playing netball, rounders, draughts and darts.

She played board games with Curie almost every night. But the games themselves were never the important thing. It was the time spent playing them which mattered; time spent talking, bonding, and discovering each other's quirks.

In terms of age, Curie was like a daughter to Renee. Renee felt a duty of care towards her young housemate; ruffling her hair each morning, and rushing to her assistance whenever she grazed her knee. The way Curie's freckles stretched and faded when she laughed, filled Renee with a moreish sense of affection. Curie's habit of wiping her nose on her sleeve gave Renee an inexplicable feeling of warmth.

In terms of maturity, however, Curie and Renee were more like sisters. They nattered about boys, hairstyles and the other villagers. When one of them giggled it set off a chain reaction; the other person giggled, and then the first person giggled some more. When one of them sneezed, the other usually hiccupped or burped or clapped.

Renee remained close to Simone. She copied her use of language; speaking empathetically, and calling people "My love".

But it was her relationship with the mutt man that really came out of the blue. She bonded with that hound; taking him for walks, playing *Fetch* and rubbing his belly. She stopped seeing him as a dog, as the lowdown scoundrel he was. She saw through his canine exterior, ignored his hairy torso, forgot his crooked legs and began to see his humanity.

Ugh! I don't know how she did it.

She noticed how the mutt man had individual tastes, just like anyone else; preferring beef and mutton to lamb and fish. Although he ate raw meat from the floor, since it was the only food he was given, when Renee offered him a sandwich he seemed happy to try it. He tilted his head, frowned, and slowly extended his paw; taking the sandwich and lifting it to his mouth.

He smiled, just like any other person would smile.

Whilst he didn't speak, Renee noticed the way he bounded, happily, whenever he saw her. She noticed how he lifted his head whenever he was excited, and how he shivered whenever he was cold. His eyes seemed to reveal the most human of emotions: Sadness and joy, hope and fear, surprise and disgust.

After a week, it finally hit her:

"That's it! We're not like the natives, you and me. We're outcasts: The only people to escape from London. The only ones raised elsewhere. We'll never be like the locals, my love, but we'll always be like each other. We'll always find solace in our shared adventures. I know it. I just know it. We're meant to be a team!"

The mutt man wagged his bottom and nodded his head. I could almost smell the foul odour in his fur; that repugnant stench of manure and rotting ham. It made me want to choke.

But, I'm afraid to say, this statement was no one-off. Comments like this became the norm. Whenever Renee saw that wretched beast, her nostrils opened and she sucked him in. Her heart jumped. Her visions blurred, then cleared, then blurred. She sighed, simpered, and smiled with all her might.

Ugh! I mean, yuck! I couldn't understand it at all.

I decided it was time to act...

***

A crow landed on the windowsill.

Renee had to blink several times before she recognized it. She had to blink several more times before she saw the note attached to its foot.

She opened the window and removed the note:

You are cordially invited to tea with Paul Podsicle the Second at Knebworth House. A drone will collect you at noon.

Renee tutted. She'd only just arrived in the village, was settled, and had no desire to leave. She drank some camomile tea, combed her hair and clipped her nails.

She remembered Chomsky's speech:

"What had he said?... Hmm... Oh yes: '*We always answered the oligarch's calls, because we feared he'd send us to London if we refused*'."

Renee felt her body weight increase by several tonnes. Her feet pressed into the ground, she was unable to lift her thighs, and was sure her chair would collapse at any moment:

"If I refuse to go, Paul Podsicle might expel the entire village.

And then what? These people couldn't survive in London. They're not equipped for individualistic life. I'd be... Oh... Oh... *Oh...*"

Renee held her head in her hands and prayed for the table to swallow her whole.

Simone, who had just seen the note, massaged her shoulders:

"It's horrible, isn't it? But you really don't have to go if you don't want to. It's okay, my love, it's okay."

But it wasn't okay. Renee *did* have to go, even though she didn't want to.

It was the biggest challenge she had faced. Yes, coming off her gas, removing her Plenses and leaving London had been hard. But she'd done that for herself. Her pain had been softened by her faith; by her belief that she was going to escape her troubled existence, find 'Mum', find freedom, and start a new life afresh. It was a case of *Lots of pain. Lots of gain.*

This was different. This was a case of *Lots of pain. No gain.* Renee could lose everything: Her friends, home and happiness. But she had nothing to gain herself.

"We'll understand," Simone continued, although the look in her eyes betrayed her. Her eyelids had retreated into her skull and her pupils had grown to double their normal size.

Renee shook her head:

"I wouldn't be able to live with myself if I stayed. I... I... I have to go. I mean, what's the worst that could happen? Right? You guys have gone before. I'm sure it'll be fine."

Curie ran up to Renee, jumped on her lap, kissed her cheek and squeezed her as hard as she could.

***

The whole village turned out to wave Renee goodbye.

She watched them, fading to dots, as the drone rose upwards and shot off at lightning speed.

Beneath her, the overgrown fields, young forests and veiny streams blurred into a mush of green and blue. Renee tried to remember each road she passed, although this was easier said than done. Her head began to spin.

She was lightheaded by the time she arrived. She stepped out from the drone and tumbled to the floor.

A robot helped her to her feet, dusted her down, and led her to Knebworth House; a fifteenth century mansion, as wide as the eye could see, which was decorated with a farrago of turrets and domes; merlons, gargoyles and flags. It was yellow-beige, with tall windows, arched doors, and the sort of gravitas that only ever comes with age.

The main doors swung open and Renee stepped inside.

She shivered with déjà vu.

She felt that she'd already visited that giant space, with its lavish red carpets and crystal chandeliers, but couldn't remember when. She recognised this ruby-encrusted sofa and this gilded piano, these figurines and Fabergé eggs, but couldn't remember why. She felt she was experiencing something she'd experienced before; as though she'd stepped back into another age, another world, another body and another life.

At either end of the room, tall mirrors reflected their own golden frames. Between them, a pair of shiny black doors began to open.

Renee stepped through, entered the next room, and caught sight of a man who was lounging in his throne; wearing a satin dressing gown and a pair of emerald-encrusted slippers. Renee was sure she'd viewed him before, but couldn't remember where.

This man was handsome, oh so handsome! A finer specimen, humanity has never known. He was constructed from luxury muscle: Flat-chested, broad-shouldered and long-limbed. The harsher angles of his body had been sanded down, smoothed and softened. His skin glowed; all terracotta, silk and enamel. He was frightfully clean, as though he'd been pampered, groomed, manicured and massaged on an almost hourly basis.

He raised his glass.

Renee stepped forward:

"Heh... Heh... Hello?"

Bada-bing! Just to hear her! Just to see her in the flesh! My heart skipped several beats.

I looked into her eyes and grinned:

"Beloved Renee: Don't just stand there. Come, take a seat. Make yourself at home."

***

"Beloved," Renee thought. "*Be... Love... Ed*. Now, where have I listened to that word before?"

She was sitting in one of Queen Victoria's chairs, trying to make sense of the situation. Her hair reflected my chandeliers; sparkling, as if infused with fireflies and fairy lights. It took all the strength at my disposal to stop myself from reaching out, grabbing her, and planting my lips onto hers.

"Do I... Umm... Know you?"

That look of intense mental exertion! Beloved friend: She positively glowed!

I pinched my thigh and tried to keep my cool, although I can't say I succeeded:

"I do believe my avatars have had the pleasure of your company."

Renee opened her mouth to speak. She paused. I trembled.

"Come on," I told myself. "You can do this."

I took a deep breath and sank back into my chair, allowing Renee to find her words:

"Podsicle?"

I nodded.

"Oxford Circus?"

I smiled.

"Interviewer..."

Renee stopped, ran her eyes along my Van Goghs, Picassos and Rembrandts; passed a couple of moments in silent contemplation, and finally turned around.

Kerching! My heart skipped another beat.

Renee bit her lower lip:

"They say you own a quarter of Britain."

"A quarter!" I scoffed. "No. Ho, ho, ho! How people exaggerate. No, my sweet, I barely own a fifth."

"Oh."

"I own a quarter of Africa."

"Oh. What's that like?"

"I can't say for certain. I've never been."

Renee raised her eyebrows.

I handed her a flute of champagne:

"Tell me your story. I'm ever so keen to hear it."

She smiled! She positively beamed! I wanted to fist-pump the air and do a kooky dance.

I'm happy to say I did not.

I held myself rigid and listened as Renee talked about her Eureka Moment, how she'd spoken to the rats, crushed her hairclip and removed her Plenses.

She paused, looked up, and gazed into the deepest depths of my eyes.

I don't know what I did, I hadn't said a word, but something must have given me away. For Renee gripped hold of her chair, lifted herself a little, and spoke out with brazen authority:

"You know all this already!!!"

I was taken aback, but did my best not to show it.

I nodded.

She continued:

"But... How?"

I smiled:

"I've been taking care of you for a long time, my sweet. Don't you remember those jobs my avatars gave you? I paid you the money you needed to survive. Without me, your debt would've been unmanageable, you'd have lost your pod and your medicine would've been disconnected."

"That happened!"

"But only once you were ready."

"Ready... How on earth did you know I'd be ready?"

She had me bang to rights. My love subsided, for the briefest of moments; replaced by a stomach-dropping sense of disquiet.

It didn't last long. Before I could find my bearings, I found myself respecting her gumption, and loving her more than before.

I considered honesty to be the best policy:

"You'd proved yourself already. In the name of the market, you had!"

Renee gestured for me to continue.

"I took you to Podsicle Palace, to show you true wealth; to help you to realise how little you had, even though you worked so hard. And I gave you a job offer, to wake you up early, when your gas was light, so you could assess your situation with a clear mind. I helped you to see the sheer futility of your existence."

"But... But... But how did you know that'd work?"

"I didn't! Ho, ho, ho. Dear Renee: The first seventy-five times, it didn't work at all. I bet you don't remember those mornings? You inhaled so much medicine, you wiped your memory clean."

Renee shook her head:

"Hang on. If it didn't work seventy-five times, why did you keep trying?"

"Because you kept trying!

"Each time you woke early, you saw the same images and had the same thoughts. You realised you'd never repay your debt, own your pod, retire, be happy or free. Anyone else would've killed themselves there and then. But not you! Oh no. You came to that nasty realisation on no less than seventy-six different occasions, and each time you saved yourself. Not just once, not just twice, but seventy-six times! Bravo! That, my sweet, is how I knew you were special."

Renee shook her head:

"No! No, no, no! It can't be true. If I'd experienced that before, I-Green would've remembered and helped me through."

I shrugged:

"I wiped your avatars clean."

"You... Wiped... Them... Clean?"

"Yes. Your avatars worked for me. I owned them, since you hadn't repaid your debt."

I smiled:

"Beloved Renee: I've been observing you for years; watching you through your avatars' eyes. I've always been by your side. Always! I know you as well as I know myself. And I tell you this: I love you *even more* than I love myself."

"You... You... You can't do that. It's spying! It's an invasion of privacy!"

This comment shook me to my core:

"Oh Renee! Please believe me: I never wanted to hurt you."

Renee ground her teeth:

"But... So... So, what changed?"

"On the seventy-sixth time, you broke your kettle. Its remains gave you a visual trigger, which helped you to remember your revelation. Then it was a matter of patience. When you cut down on your gas, I knew we were on the right path. I just needed to take you to Mansion House, to give you a few more clues. Then I cut your gas. I knew you'd survive. You were ready.

"After that, things were easy. You worked most of it out for yourself, removed your Plenses and left Podsville. I just had to send my crow, my trusty little spy drone, who led you to South Mimms. The rest, as they say, is history."

Renee looked confused:

"But... But... Surely there was a simpler way."

I laughed. It didn't become me, I regret it now, but I positively guffawed:

"A simpler way? Of course! But if things had been simple, anyone could've made it. And I didn't want anyone. I wanted to find someone special. I wanted to find *you!*"

Renee gripped hold of my armrests:

"So... You mean... There were others?"

I nodded.

"And my mum. What about my mum? Was she one of the others?"

I tensed my cheeks, bowed my head and nodded ever so slightly.

"You... You mean... What? She... No..."

I nodded.

"She killed herself?"

I winced.

"You drove her to suicide?"

Renee had risen to her feet. She was clenching her teeth, grinding her jaw and running her nails up her arms. Her face puffed out in every direction. It wasn't a good look. And yet, I must admit, I loved her more than ever. Even in this wretched state, I still found her attractive.

What crazy, crazy love!

"But... But... I only wanted a mother. That's what this was about!"

I rose, stepped towards our Renee, put my hand on her shoulder and spoke in a soothing tone:

"No. Beloved Renee: It's regrettable, it's truly horrific. Sometimes I find it hard to sleep. But you weren't looking for your mother. This was never about her."

Taken aback by the sheer bravado of my statement, Renee struggled to respond:

"I... Wasn't... Looking... For... Mum?"

"No. You didn't want *your* mum. You wanted *to be a* mum. You want to have a baby!"

Renee's head jolted back. Her neck slowly returned it to its rightful position. Her eyelids closed to a slit, and then parted, a millimetre at a time, until her eyes began to bulge:

"I do! But... But how did you... I do! I want a baby!"

"You do! That's what this is about!

"Beloved Renee: Humanity had fallen into a state of disgrace. I needed to find one pure being, one angel, with whom I could start the race afresh. I looked high, I looked low, and then I found you. You're the one! The love of my loves! The Eve to my Adam.

"My sweet: I've spent my entire life searching for you, and now I've found you. I mean, yippee! Renee: We were born to be together. We *will* live forever, love forever, and create the most perfect heirs. The human race will be pure once again!"

I dropped to my knees, removed a diamond ring from my pocket, and held it up to my love:

"Renee Ann Blanca: Be my wife!"

Renee beamed. She positively glowed!

She held out her hand.

My dream was coming true! We were going to unite!

Snap! It happened in a heartbeat: Our Renee turned icy cold.

It made me shudder.

It made Renee retreat:

"Hang on... You... You... You drove my mum to suicide?"

I nodded:

"I'm so sorry, my sweet, but that's all in the past. It doesn't matter now."

"It matters to me!"

"I know."

"How many others did you kill?"

"Kill? Why Renee, I didn't kill anyone. Not a single soul."

"Semantics! Pure semantics! Tell me. Tell me now! How many people did you drive to suicide?"

"Most of them, I suppose. Ho, ho, ho. Some people killed themselves immediately. Others took several minutes. Everyone killed themselves in their own individual way. A few people even escaped. But those people either died in the wilderness or returned to Podsville. You were the only one who made it to South Mimms."

Renee screamed:

"The only one? Everyone else... Died? Tens of millions? Eighty million? You killed... Eighty... Million... People? You're a monster. You're... Aaagh!!!"

She threw her champagne at one of my Rembrandts, but didn't wait to see it smash. She turned, toppled Queen Victoria's chair and stormed away.

My heart was racing.

I gave chase, and yelled out with lovestruck desperation:

"Beloved Renee: You simply cannot go. You owe me one hundred and fourteen thousand pounds. One *must* repay one's debts.

It's a matter of honour. Renee! Renee! One must repay one's debts."

She was getting away, I was getting tired, but I forced myself on:

"Renee! Beloved Renee! Think of the life we could live. Think of our beautiful children."

We passed my koi carp, fountains and lawns:

"Renee! Beloved Renee! You dreamed of owning your own pod and retiring. You can do that! I can make your dream come true!"

We left my compound:

"Renee! Beloved Renee! We can go anywhere you want. You can have anything you want. We can do anything you want together.

"Renee! Beloved Renee…"

It was no good.

My sweetheart had disappeared.

The sky had turned black.

The wind was whistling with derision:

"I love someone else… Someone else… Someone else…"

HEAR ME OUT

> "The greatest deception men suffer
> is from their own opinions."
> **LEONARDO DA VINCI**

I'd like to think I've earned your sympathies. You've seen the extraordinary lengths I've gone to in search of love, and you've seen how I was rejected in the cruellest of ways. Never, in the history of humankind, has anyone given so much only to receive so little.

I'd like to think you're with me, feeling my heartbreak, as I cry these tears of love:

My Renee! Beloved Renee! Why have you forsaken me?

Alas, I cannot be sure. Your generation is a little different to mine. I fear you may have judged me harshly.

It's because I drove eighty million people to suicide, isn't it? You're judging me for that.

DON'T! It doesn't become you.

I didn't kill anyone. NOT A SINGLE SOUL! Can you get that into your head?

Everyone is free. That's the thing with individualism: Everyone is free to be whoever they want to be. There's no authoritarian state; no *Big Brother* or *Resident World Controller*. Everyone is free! Everyone defines themselves, through the market; working as hard as they like, doing whatever jobs they choose, and consuming the products that make them truly unique. No king or prime minister can get in their way. They're their own king, their own prime minister. They control the narrative. THEY CHOOSE!

I didn't kill anyone. Not a single soul. How could I? Those people were free to act in any way they chose. So what if they chose to kill themselves? It was *their* decision, not mine.

But I'll tell you this: Their behaviour was truly delightful. The ultimate act of freedom. Not only did they take personal responsibility for their lives, they also took personal responsibility for their deaths. Thatcher would've been so proud. Those people *got on their bikes*.

What? You don't believe me? You blame me from driving them to their deaths? Really? Aaagh! Your generation is so perverse.

Oh yes, I bet you think you're perfect, sitting there reading this memoir. But why? Because you've never driven anyone to suicide? Well whoop-dee-doo.

Look: I only ever followed the rules of the game. It was *your* generation who wrote those rules. You privatised industry, crushed the unions, destroyed society and forced everyone to compete. YOU created this Individutopia. YOU drove eighty million people to their deaths.

Actions have consequences. When a fireman enters a blaze, he knows he may be burned. When an antelope grazes in a meadow, she knows she may be eaten.

When your generation told people to take personal responsibility for their lives, you were telling them to take personal responsibility for their deaths. You were putting a knife in their hands and telling them to use it.

Don't blame me. Who was I to argue with the world I was born into? We oligarchs are beholden to the rules of individualism, just like everyone else; compelled to act in our own self-interest, as the true individuals we are.

All I wanted was love. Can you really despise me for that? What sort of a monster are you?

I'll tell you this again: I only wanted to love and be loved.

Is that really so wrong? Isn't that what *you* want? Isn't that what *we all* want?

Aargh!!!

Look at what happened to me. Just look at what happened!

I spent my whole life running algorithms, training avatars, testing tens of millions of people. I spent all day, every day, searching for my one true love.

I suffered defeat on an hourly basis. It was agony incarnate. But victory was so much worse.

I found my one true love: Our Renee. She came to me, sat in this chair, drank this champagne and breathed this air. We were going to be happy, oh so happy.

And then what? Then she left me! It was all over before it began.

Renee judged me for my actions, without considering my intentions. She took my love and replaced it with hate.

Think of me! Just think of me!

You should be crying my tears, feeling my pain. You should be broken-hearted, clutching your ribs, rolling around on your bedroom floor.

Beloved Renee, my Renee, my love!

Come back. Hear me out. You'll understand me if you give me a chance. You'll be happy. We'll be happy together.

Renee, oh Renee, my love.

EPILOGUE

"What? There's more?"
JOSS SHELDON

~~Dear Diary,~~

No. That simply won't do.

It's been five years since Renee sat in this chair. Five years, filled with pain, sorrow and remorse. Five years, in which I've done my best to recover.

I was hoping I'd have more chapters to write, that Renee would have a change of heart and return to my loving arms.

Alas, things haven't been so kind.

I've forced myself to re-watch my recordings of Renee, to observe her with a fresh set of eyes. Talking to you, whilst watching these videos, has really helped me to heal. Believe it or not, you're the only human company I have.

Thank-you! Your presence has been a great source of comfort.

With your help, I feel ready to finish this tale; to accept it's not about me, it was never about me, it was always about your Renee.

Inhale. Exhale. Inhale.

Let's see what we can do…

***

My crow, my trusty spy drone, followed Renee home from Knebworth House. She'd done well to remember the route, and returned without stopping to rest.

I wanted to give chase. I wanted to destroy her entire village.

I couldn't do it. I couldn't hurt anyone who made your Renee happy.

God, I wanted to kill them!

I couldn't do it. I felt compelled to respect Renee's choice.

She arrived in South Mimms, ignored everyone she passed, and ran straight into the paws of that horrible, horrible mutt. Can you believe it? Ugh! It makes me shudder just to think of that naked beast. I had everything, he had nothing, and yet Renee chose him over me! Do you now understand why I hate him so much?

Aaagh!

Renee squealed as soon as she saw that pitiful dog:

"Everything's brighter when I'm with you. We're the only two of our kind: Abandoned and then found. I love you Darwin. We're meant to be together."

They hugged and wrestled and licked each other's flesh. Then it happened. Beloved friend: If you're of a sensitive disposition, I suggest you look away.

Renee ripped off her clothes, revealing her beautiful body; tightened from years of hard work, but untouched by any man. She got down on her hands and knees, lifted her rear end, and smiled with blissful contentment.

That nasty mutt jumped up onto his hind legs, placed his paws on her back and thrust himself into her body.

My crow flew away.

I couldn't bear to watch.

***

A decade-long study, conducted in the 1980s, found that men who kissed their wives in the morning lived five years longer than men who did not. They earned twenty percent more and were a third less likely to die in a car accident. It all came down to their mental state: Their morning kiss put them in a positive frame of mind, which helped them to succeed.

Renee kissed the mutt man as soon as they awoke. They never stopped kissing. It made her so happy, so positive, so damn effervescent. I tell you: She glistened.

It made my stomach turn.

But there was a silver lining. Each time I watched them kiss, I choked and gagged and retched. Wishing to wipe that sordid memory from my mind, I was unable to return to my spying.

The more they kissed, the less time I spent watching your Renee. I weaned myself away from my screen.

A part of me thought Renee was doing it on purpose; sending me a message whenever she noticed my crow:

"I love someone else... Someone else... Someone else..."

But whether it was intentional or not, one thing was beyond doubt: It worked. It helped me to conquer my addiction.

I've found alternative outlets for my pent-up energy; taking the time I used to spend spying, and using it to hike or fish. I've adopted a cat, Cherry, who gives me the companionship I so desperately need. I've even considered visiting South Mimms, although I've been unable to muster the courage.

These days, I can go for weeks without stalking Renee. I still think of her every day, but the memories don't chafe. The wounds have almost healed.

***

I'll leave you with what little information I have. I wish I could tell you more. But how can I, when I hardly ever spy on your Renee? This, I'm afraid to say, is as much as I know…

Renee is happy. I hope it pleases you to learn this.

Whenever there's a wedding, she smiles so hard it hurts. She dances whenever there's music and participates in all the community's events; celebrating the solstices, praying for rain, and organising the harvest festivities.

She's integrated into village life, which still follows the same old routine. For sure, there have been skirmishes: Kropotkin falsely accused Kuti of poisoning his sheep. A married man committed adultery. A young girl stole a spear. But such disputes were soon resolved in the longhouse: Kropotkin lashed himself, the adulterer's wife was granted a divorce and the girl made three new spears. Things returned to normal.

If one thing did change, however, it was the villagers' attitude to the mutt man. They'd been quick to judge Renee when she first made love to that thing; accusing her of "Bestiality" and "Public indecency". A few villagers had submitted a motion for them to be expelled. But that motion was rejected when Curie came to the mutt man's defence; pointing out the way he helped to find mushrooms and truffles, how he protected the village, and how he was becoming slightly more human each day.

Renee taught the mutt man to eat human food, from a plate, at a specially constructed table. Whilst he still crawled on all fours, he began to shower himself, voluntarily, and comb his own hair. He couldn't form sentences, but Renee did teach him some words: "Simone", "Bedtime" and "Apple". He learned sign language. He voted during village debates, peeled vegetables and took charge of the household's fire.

He became a dad!

Renee gave birth to twins: A boy and a girl. She called them her "Puppies", breastfed them whilst lying on her side, and taught them to both bark and speak.

I was right about that: Renee *did* want to be a mum. She wanted to mother every child in the village. She wanted to babysit them, take them for walks, and play with them whenever she could.

She began to teach in the village school; a collection of four classrooms, which smelled of waxy floorboards and PVA glue. After a year as a teacher's assistant, she was given her own class. Within three years, she'd created her own course.

Yes, that's correct. Renee wrote a textbook: "Individutopia: A Warning From History".

She held lectures in the longhouse, teaching about the perils of individualism, personal responsibility and hard work. She shocked children and adults alike with her tales of working for the sake of working, chasing impossible dreams and ignoring other people.

She'd finally found her niche.

***

I spied on Renee for the last time a couple of months ago. I don't plan to do it again. So I suppose it makes sense for me to leave you with a brief account of what happened on that sunny, autumn day...

***

Curie had become an inquisitive teen, with terrible acne and hair that reached her waist. She'd formed her own group of ramblers, who often gathered more leaves and berries than Simone's. And she was a bit of a scholar. She'd attended all Renee's lectures, read her book seven times, and knew more about individualism than anyone else from South Mimms.

It was unsurprising, then, that it was Curie who asked the question:

"Renee: Will you take us to London?"

Tongues began to wag. And yet, despite the rumbling undercurrent of disapproval, Curie still managed to recruit eight intrepid explorers. They met by the service station at dawn, wearing the village's sturdiest boots, and carrying backpacks filled with clothes, blankets, food, torches and homemade gas masks.

Renee led them on, returning the way she'd come all those years before.

As soon as they climbed down from the motorway, she had to hug one young pilgrim and tell her she was going to be okay. As soon as they reached Barnet, she had to address the entire group:

"No one said this would be easy. But you can be heroes: The first Socialists in Individutopia. You'll be legends in South Mimms. The talk of the village! And I tell you this: You'll be safe. If I could escape on my own, you'll be fine together. You've got nothing to lose but your fear."

There was a brief moment of silence. Then Curie began to sing "Redemption Song", the others joined in, and they all marched down the road; singing song after song, whilst traipsing through Whetstone Stray, Highgate Golf Club and Hampstead Heath.

Renee spoke in a nostalgic tone:

"This is where I spent my first ever night of freedom."

Everyone roared:

"Three cheers for Renee! Hip-hip, hooray!"

Renee blushed.

She sat down by the pond, opened her bag, and passed some sandwiches to her team.

She was overcome by doubt:

"What if I can't leave? What if I don't want to leave? What if I'm made to pay my debt?"

These thoughts soon disappeared.

She smiled.

She'd seen Curie, with mayonnaise smeared across her face,

and the mutt man, who was swimming in the pond. She unpacked her cards and began to play.

***

It was mid-afternoon by the time they reached Tottenham Court Road.

There wasn't another soul in sight. Only the wind made a sound; gushing between empty buildings, tapping their windows and rattling their doors. The rats were eerily quiet.

The smog was thick, acrid and bitter.

Renee removed her gas mask, only to see that her companions were already wearing theirs. They were made from some old plastic bottles, and some wool, which Kropotkin had sheared that summer. They looked a little ridiculous, but they worked a treat.

"This is the West End Industrial Estate," Renee explained. "And this is Oxford Street. In the old days, this road was filled with 'Shops': Places where people bought clothes, toys and accessories."

She could hear the murmurs: "Bought". "Shops". "Accessories".

"This is the Visa Tower and this is the Samsung Column. Up ahead, you can just about see Oxford Circus. That's where I met the Podsicle Interviewer. It was the Podsicle Interviewer who sent me to Podsicle Palace, where I began to break free."

Curie jumped up and down:

"Renee! Please, Renee! Can we go to Podsicle Palace? Please, Renee, please!"

Renee laughed:

"Okay, my love, follow me."

They headed down Saint George Street, Bruton Lane and Berkeley Street; trying hard not to inhale too deeply, and trying harder not to trip over the litter.

Renee's friends were unsure how to react to the tall, glassy towers, which reached up on either side; stealing the sky and turning it green. They felt an urge to run inside, and an even greater urge to keep their distance. This world was so new to them, so vain, that it made them shudder in time.

Renee could sense their discomfort.

"It's okay," she said. "It's enough to look on from afar."

Her team exhaled as one.

But they weren't nearly so awed by Podsicle Palace. The fact it was made of stone, a natural substance, seemed to put their minds at ease. When Renee stepped inside, her teammates were happy to follow.

They spent hours in that place, pretending to be kings, queens, princes, jesters, courtesans, servants and slaves. They ran around, with portraits held in front of their faces. They sat in the royal throne, wore the crown jewels, played the pianos and took two souvenirs: A nodding figurine and a Chinese dragon.

By the time they left, the sky was solid black. They lit their torches and headed through town.

"I promised you a night in Podsville," Renee declared. "And I always keep my promises."

Curie cheered:

"Renee: Can we really sleep in our own pod?"

"Oh yes."

"And if we find it scary, can we come and sleep with you?"

"Of course, my love, of course!"

***

They'd just passed the Monument to the Invisible Hand, when they came across the beggar. His trousers had faded. It'd be wrong to call them brown, just as it'd be wrong to call them white. They were colourless. *The man* was colourless. Both he and his clothes had melted into the background.

Renee's companions walked by, oblivious to his existence, but Renee came to a halt. She'd seen her image, reflected in the beggar's shoes, and had recognised his braid. Even though his face had wrinkled, like a raisin; even though his features had been sucked in towards his nose; even though he looked older and frailer than anyone Renee had ever seen; he still reminded her of herself, and the life she used to lead.

She saw the star-shaped birthmark on his lower lip.

"Oh yes," she thought. "Oh no."

She hadn't thought of that man for years. Perhaps her mind had blocked him out. Perhaps. But here she was, stood before him, unable to deny his existence, certain he was alive, and certain he needed her help:

"But... But, how?... How have you survived here alone?"

The man's eyelids were stuck together with residue and dust. His lips were glued together with dried saliva. Renee had no option but to wait, patiently, as he struggled to pry them open.

After several minutes, a small gap appeared at the side of his mouth. This gap began to spread, unzipping his lips an atom at a time.

The man whispered so softly, and gasped so much, that Renee had to hold her ear to his mouth to hear him:

"Rah... Rah... Ah... Is that you?... Ah... It's so nice to hear another voice."

Renee repeated her question:

"My love: How have you survived here alone?"

The man licked his lips:

"I... Ah... I've never been a part of this... Ah... I've never had avatars... Ah... I scavenge for food... I eat rats if I'm lucky."

Renee's heart sank.

"Why didn't I save him?" she asked herself. "Why didn't I come back to help?"

The man was trying to speak:

"Rah... Rah... Renee?... Ah... Is that you?"

Renee stumbled:

"How... How did you know my name?"

The man tried to smile. His cheeks rose a little, then collapsed:

"You're... My... Renee?... Ah... My angel!"

Renee frowned.

The man managed to smile:

"My Renee?... Ah... My princess?... Ah... My girl!"

He was struggling to open his eyes:

"I never wanted to leave you... Ah... Never... But what was I to do?... Ah... Your mother dumped you... Ah... My sweet girl... When I found you, you couldn't hear or see me... Ah... But I never gave up... I made it my mission to call to you each day... Ah... I vowed I'd stay here till the end of time... Ah... My princess... My Renee... My girl!"

Tears cascaded down Renee's cheeks:

"Da... Dad? Is that you?"

The man prised open his eyes:

"Renee!"

"Dad!"

"Renee!"

"Dad!"

Renee smiled with Herculean might, before passing her father a cinnamon bun:

"Dad: We're going to take you home, okay? We have a lovely village, with lots of food and lots of friends. My love: We'll nurse you back to health."

Her father closed his eyes.

"Dad?"

His head fell forwards.

"Dad???"

His torso went limp and collapsed.

"Dad! Dad! You can't leave me now! Not after all these years. Not after it's taken so long to find you!"

Renee shook her father, gently, and tried to pry open his eyes. She kept saying "Dad! Dad!" She massaged, rubbed and pinched him:

"Oh Renee! How could I leave him so long?"

She searched for a pulse, for a breath, for any sign of life.

She kept looking, more in hope than expectation.

She recalled the masturbating man, and how she'd mocked him every day. She recalled the beggar, and how she'd left him without uttering a word.

She crumpled into a ball, yanked her hair, cried herself dry, waited for minutes and waited for hours.

Curie pulled her away.

"He's passed on," she said in a sombre hush. "It's okay, it's okay. Let's get you to bed. We'll bury him tomorrow. My sister: There's nothing you can do."

Renee rubbed a tear from her cheek:

"Goodbye, sweet daddy, farewell. I'm so sorry I didn't come before. But if you can hear me now, wherever you are, I want you to know that I love you. I've always loved you. You'll always be my daddy."

She arose, shakily, all too aware of her kneecaps, which were rubbing against her bones.

A rat scurried by.

The wind whistled.

A faint sound caressed Renee's ear:

"Rah... Rah... Renee... Ah... My daughter... Ah... Don't worry, I'm fine... Ah... Come, my girl, take me home..."

DEMOCRACY

A USER'S GUIDE

THEY SAY WE LIVE IN A DEMOCRACY. WE ARE FREE AND WE SHOULD BE GRATEFUL.

But just how "Free" are we? How democratic are our so-called "Democracies"?

Is it enough to simply elect our leaders and sit back, helpless, as they rule over us like dictators? What good is selecting our politicians, if we cannot control our media, police or soldiers? If we must blindly follow our teachers' and bosses' commands, whilst at school and in the workplace, is it not a little naïve to believe that we are the masters of our own destinies? And if our resources are controlled by a tiny cabal of plutocrats, bankers and corporations; can we honestly say that our economies are being run for us?

Could things not be a little bit more, well, democratic?

Indeed they can! "Democracy: A User's Guide" shows us how...

Within the pages of this story-filled book, we shall visit Summerhill, a democratic school in the east of England, before stopping off in Brazil to check out Semco, where workplace democracy is the name of the game. We will travel to Rojava, to explore life in a democratic army, and head to Spain, to see why Podemos is giving liquid democracy a go. We shall travel back in time, to see democracy at work in hunter-gatherer societies, tribal confederacies, the guilds and on the commons. We will consider the case for participatory budgeting, deliberative democracy, collaborative hiring, community currencies, peer-to-peer lending, and much much more.

The message is clear and concise: Democracy does not have to be a pipe dream. We have all the tools we need to rule ourselves.

MONEY POWER LOVE

ALL WARS ARE BANKERS' WARS

"Breathtaking"
The Huffington Post
"Picaresque"
Scottish Left Review
"Unputdownable"
The Avenger
"Strangely kind"
The Tribune

Born on three adjacent beds, a mere three seconds apart, our three heroes are united by nature but divided by nurture. As a result of their different upbringings, they spend their lives chasing three very different things: Money, power and love.

This is a human story: A tale about people like ourselves, cajoled by the whimsy of circumstance, who find themselves performing the most beautiful acts as well as the most vulgar.

This is a historical story: A tale set in the early 1800s, which shines a light on how bankers, with the power to create money out of nothing, were able to shape the world we live in today.

And this is a love story: A tale about three men, who fall in love with the same woman, at the very same time...

THE LITTLE VOICE

Can you remember who you were before the world told you who you should be?

"The most thought-provoking novel of 2016"
The Huffington Post
"Radical... A masterclass... Top notch..."
The Canary
"A pretty remarkable feat"
BuzzFeed

Dear reader,

My character has been shaped by two opposing forces; the pressure to conform to social norms, and the pressure to be true to myself. To be honest with you, these forces have really torn me apart. They've pulled me one way and then the other. At times, they've left me questioning my whole entire existence.

But please don't think that I'm angry or morose. I'm not. Because through adversity comes knowledge. I've suffered, it's true. But I've learnt from my pain. I've become a better person.

Now, for the first time, I'm ready to tell my story. Perhaps it will inspire you. Perhaps it will encourage you to think in a whole new way. Perhaps it won't. There's only one way to find out...

Enjoy the book,

Yew Shodkin

ALSO BY JOSS SHELDON...

OCCUPIED

SOME PEOPLE LIVE UNDER OCCUPATION
SOME PEOPLE OCCUPY THEMSELVES
NO ONE IS FREE

"A unique piece of literary fiction"
The Examiner
"Candid and disquieting"
Free Tibet
"Genre-busting"
Pak Asia Times

Step into a world which is both magically fictitious and shockingly real, to follow the lives of Tamsin, Ellie, Arun and Charlie; a refugee, native, occupier and economic migrant. Watch them grow up during a halcyon past, everyday present and dystopian future. And be prepared to be amazed.

Inspired by the occupations of Palestine, Kurdistan and Tibet, and by the corporate occupation of the west, 'Occupied' is a haunting glance into a society which is a little too familiar for comfort. It truly is a unique piece of literary fiction...

INVOLUTION & EVOLUTION

This is the story of Alfred Freeman, a boy who does everything he can; to serve humankind. He feeds five-thousand youths, salves-saves-and-soothes; and champions the maligned. He helps paralytics to feel fine, turns water into wine; and gives sight to the blind.

When World War One draws near, his nation is plunged into fear; and so Alfred makes a stand. He opposes the war and calls for peace, disobeys the police; and speaks out across the land. He makes speeches, and he preaches; using statements which sound grand.

But the authorities hit back, and launch a potent-attack; which is full of disgust-derision-and-disdain. Alfred is threatened with execution, and suffers from persecution; which leaves him writhing in pain. He struggles to survive, remain alive; keep cool and stay sane.

'Involution & Evolution' is a masterpiece of rhyme, with a message which echoes through time; and will get inside your head. With colourful-characters and poetic-flair, it is a scathing critique of modern-warfare; and all its gory-bloodshed. It's a novel which breaks new ground, is sure to astound; and really must be read.

www.joss-sheldon.com

BE THE ONE OF THE FIRST PEOPLE TO FIND OUT ABOUT JOSS SHELDON'S NEXT NOVEL. SIGN UP FOR HIS NEWSLETTER TODAY...

http://joss-sheldon.com/newsletter/4592876008

If you enjoyed this book, please leave a review online.
Joss Sheldon does not have a professional marketing team behind him – he needs your help to spread the word about his books!

9-23

Made in the USA
Middletown, DE
27 November 2020

25242519R00104